Curse of Gold

Jack Mould and the
Curse of Gold

Elizabeth Hawkins

hancock

house

ISBN 0-88839-281-8
Copyright © 1993 Jack Mould

2nd printing

Cataloging in Publication Data
Hawkins, Elizabeth M., 1942–
Jack Mould and the curse of gold

ISBN 0-88839-281-8

1. Gold mines and mining—British Columbia—Pitt
Lake Region—History. 2. Slumach, d. 1891. 3. Mould,
Jack, 1936– 4. Gold miners—British Columbia—Biogra-
phy. I. Title.
TN424.C32B753 1993 622'.3422'0971137 C91-091393-5

Edited: Myron Shutty
Production: Lorna Lake

Published simultaneously in Canada and the United States by

HANCOCK HOUSE PUBLISHERS LTD.
19313 Zero Avenue, Surrey, B.C. V4P 1M7
(604) 538-1114   Fax (604) 538-2262

HANCOCK HOUSE PUBLISHERS
1431 Harrison Avenue, Box 959, Blaine, WA 98231-0959
(206) 354-6953   Fax (604) 538-2262

Contents

Introduction

I like mystery. I love murder. I've never committed one, so far. But then there may come that day when I find the lid off the peanut butter jar, and the bread crumbs left on the kitchen counter once too often.

I do read about murder. And I do write about murder—writing mystery suspense novels you see, does require a body here and there, to pique the reader's interest. A run in a stocking or a nasty hangnail simply won't do it. And along with a cadaver, one has to have a villain or two, a few characters as worker bees, and one reasonably redeemable soul who surfaces in the end to tie up the intrigue and satisfy the reader.

One day, I met Jack. He was knee deep in conversation with my husband David Hancock, discussing a book proposal. I might as well have been a fly on the wall. From my point of view, these discussions can get quite tedious, if the book in question happens to be a guide book for instance. How many species of prairie chickens should be included with hawks, owls, and pheasants? Or does seaweed get lumped in with coral, nematodes, and algae?

This conversation however, was taking on all the aspects of a thriller. As Jack's story began to unfold, I began to discover a treasury of mystery, suspense, and danger. There were characters that were unique and colorful; moral and corrupt. There was historical drama, and a remote and dangerous location. There was mystery, there was murder, there was mayhem. And there were bodies. By every conceivable turn of fate. By hanging, accident, suicide, homicide, and even massacre.

And there was Jack. As the leading larger-than-life character in real life, it soon became obvious that he was quite the lovable rogue indeed. Therefore, it took little persuasion on their part, for me to agree to take on the task of converting his story to print.

I have also departed from the main story into lightly educational vignettes and profiles for the benefit of the reader, in order that he may be offered a more informed platform to appreciate and empathize with the related topic or events.

Through many hours of taped conversations over the past two years, I have endeavored to trace his story from his childhood beginnings, through the many years of his endless search for the elusive lost gold mine. Jack has had to dig back through the cobwebs of memory to recall so many of the incidents that lead him to persevere in his quest. As accurately as possible, I have documented the details and the dates of his life and the historical background of the infamous legendary lost gold mine.

At this time of writing, it is a book without an ending. But the ending when it does come, promises to be as mysterious and intriguing as the beginning. It is a fascinating story of hardship, danger, despair, and triumph. And it is a tale as rich in color, and fascination as the very gold of the elusive legendary mine itself. Jack's story is a true story. Most of what you will read is fact, documented fact. Where answers remain unknown, I tried to hypothesize what may have occurred, using I hope, reason, logic, and the factor of probability. Some readers may wish to disagree with my interpretation but that is the nature of a tale as strange as this.

One person alone cannot take credit for the writing and production of a book. There are many people along the way who, after it's born, help care, feed, and nurture it along the way. Some will be acknowledged. Some will remain nameless. Some contribute as part of their jobs and some contribute above and beyond the call of duty. Others contribute out of interest, compassion, and friendship. Writing a book as all authors know is often a painfully long and solitary procedure. A brief flash of literary genius often ends up at the bottom of the bird cage. A single sentence can be an hour-long labor of love, paragraphs can takes days of dovetailing detail after detail, and chapters, weeks of frustrating reworking, polishing, moving, and refining. From start to finish a book usually takes longer than conception, gestation, and delivery of a child. Spiritually at least, the results are certainly as joyful.

First, I must thank my husband David, for his ever present confidence and support in my abilities as a writer. I thank the editors and staff of Hancock House Publishers for their endless time, attention to detail, and help. As an editor, Herb was uncompromising in his attention to content, and fact, gently encouraging a better word, phrase, structure or continuity. Lorna was outstanding in planning and designing a book to attain as high interest and overall appeal as possible. Diane maintained close interest and support for the book she would ultimately advertise and promote, a very necessary component in sales and marketing in the book publishing industry.

There is my agent, George, in New York who has worked closely with me for the past seven years whose confidence and encouragement was greatly appreciated. There is my long time dear and nonwriting friend Penny, whose nightly midnight call, would unerringly begin, not with a salutation but with "And the word count now is?" And there is my writer friend Tom who, with his deepest concern being that one day out of courtesy of the friendship would be obliged to read this book, took it upon himself to red pencil his editorial remarks and suggestions for which I have come to know and appreciate are excellent. Thank you David, Herb, Lorna, Diane. Thank you Penny. Thank you Tom. From the bottom of my heart.

As for Pussywillow, my black Himalayan cat, I suppose she deserves some credit too. After all, she sat on Jack's lap for hours and purred into the mike. That must count for something. Elevator music perhaps? And she sat in my lap for hours on end while I was at the keyboard. I don't think she liked the part about Sam the mouse though. Jealousy, I suppose. Twice I caught her in the pretense of rolling over and yawning, while furtively reaching out with a paw to the delete key.

ELIZABETH HAWKINS

1

Fire Mountain

Jack Mould surveyed the scene of blackened desolation with a mixture of both shock and disbelief. Three days earlier, this had been the site of a bustling mining camp. His camp. Now his hopes and his ambitions had been turned to nothing more than ashes.

The entire camp site had been destroyed. A raging forest fire had engulfed it, then furthering the destruction, a massive explosion had completed the holocaust.

For hundreds of yards in every direction, a virgin forest had been annihilated. Some trees had barely been scorched, others had burned to the bone. Still others, some of them massive Douglas firs lay beside their graves, where they had been blown out of the ground.

Jack knew why.

A forty-five gallon drum of fuel had been stored at this site, along with several boxes of ammunition. No sign of these remained.

Clearly, the drum and ammo had exploded in an inferno of destructive fury, sending balls of flames in every direction.

The heat must have been unbelievable, heat hot enough to melt steel.

Great puddles of metal were all that identified his power saws. Rifles, shotguns, and handguns had fused together in a warped and twisted heap. But amongst the debris were curious remnants of what had somehow escaped the inferno. Some distance away, the drill rig had not burned entirely, but the throttle and the needle valve were utterly destroyed. Jack had left his prospector's pick ax embedded in a tree. This tree was now a charred stump, but the pick ax with its paper label and leather thong handle survived unscathed. Yet only a few feet away, a power saw had been melted down to an almost unrecognizable lump. And by some miracle, a nearby propane tank, itself damaged by the fire, had not exploded. It still contained 100 pounds of propane.

In all, including the expense of moving everything to the site by helicopter, the fire had destroyed over 30,000 dollars worth of supplies and equipment.

None of it was insured.

The initial shock that had confronted Jack quickly turned to anger. Then as he wandered over to where he remembered his tent had been, the anger gave way to an overwhelming sense of futility and despair. Nothing whatever indicated there had ever been a tent. Yet lying in the ashes he saw the coil springs that had been inside his mattress.

He laughed.

It was a bitter laugh. The remains of the bed in which he had slept many a restless night, reminded him how fortunate he had been not to have been sleeping in it the night of the fire.

Along with his three partners, Jack had flown back to Vancouver by helicopter for a week's R and R from the backbreaking toil of searching for gold. As they had done before, many times before, they had left the camp unguarded, knowing it to be perfectly safe.

This remote and high location would never be found by anyone else, let alone be vandalized.

At least not by human trespassers. But Jack hadn't

11

counted on a bolt of lightning which, he assumed, had sparked this fire.

Once more the irony of the circumstances pointed accusingly at the shadow of the enemy that had haunted him from the beginning.

The Curse. Slumach's curse. Uttered by the Indian, seconds before he was hanged for murder 100 years ago. The curse had plagued Jack like it had the others. The same curse that was judged responsible for the death of twenty or more prospectors who had sought in vain for Slumach's legendary gold mine.

Jack believed in the gold mine. And he knew, as he had always known deep down inside of him, that he would be the one to find it.

He'd tried to ignore the curse, pass it off as rumor, superstition, a tale to be told round a campfire. But this last incident was too uncanny, too disturbing to be dismissed.

Some mysterious force seemed intent on destroying him. The closer he got to the gold, the more mishaps there seemed to be.

And something...something inside him, told him he was now very close to the gold.

Of that he was sure.

Jack thought again about the fire and the curse. Then as he pondered the lightning strike, a smile creased his weathered face. Gold is known as an excellent conductor of electricity. Right? Why, on this vast mountain, did the lightning strike where it did? Because it was attracted to the gold! Was that not confirmation of the existence of the gold mine? Right here, where he stood.

The smile dissolved into a deep rumbling laugh that echoed out and beyond the campsite. Finally, surveying the scene of desolation for the last time, he threw the surviving pickax over his shoulder, and began the long trek down to the clearing to rendezvous with the returning helicopter.

The fire had been a setback, to be sure, another in a long series of mishaps and misadventures that had plagued his life.

But it also suggested that he knew now he was close to finding the legendary Slumach gold mine he had sought for almost thirty years.

Really close.

He'd be back, and the next time, despite the CURSE, he would leave these godforsaken mountains with a fortune in gold or, like so many others who had sought their wealth and failed, he would die trying.

2
Slumach: The Legend

Molly Tynan had fourteen minutes to live. Unaware of those pitifully few moments of life slipping away, she returned to camp, her moccasined feet retracing the path she had traveled hundreds of times before. The work basket hanging from her waist was heavy, laden with the fruit of her long, arduous hours of work. Now, nearly dusk, the campfire glowed in the twilight, the flames dancing across the leathered face of the man who sat cross-legged before it, calmly anticipating the evening's ritual. With premeditated thoughts, Slumach watched her approach him.

It was time.

The evening air whispered to him of the stealthy approach of winter. Soon would come the bitter winds, the first flurries of snow, then the crippling, deadly cold and last, the white rain and ice. Of them all, it was only the snow he regarded as both friend and foe. It was his enemy, there was little doubt, for it endangered his very survival when all other risks posed little threat. But paradoxically it was also his friend, for it kept his secret safe from others who sought what he had found. No man, however desperate with greed, would risk his life in territory as brutal as this, in the dead of winter. Even in summer, those less skilled than he had lost their lives attempting to find this location. But for him, the few brief weeks of this and several past summers, had been very productive. Hidden in his caches, the rawhide bags were nearly full, enough to indulge his body and soul in an orgy of high-living pleasures in the town of New Westminster for many months, while the snow once again shrouded his secret.

Molly obediently knelt before him, and tumbled out onto a blanket the contents of her basket for his examination and approval. Deep within her, the flutterings of pleasure stirred her soul, as she too, anticipated the rewards of her hopes and dreams. Briefly her eyes rose to meet those of Slumach, who appeared to regard her with an almost wistful observance, before he turned to inspect her treasure.

Gold nuggets lay like acorns in the reflection of the flames. From tiny beads to the size of pebbles, many still wet from where they had been uncovered, washed from a main vein of inestimable wealth. Some nuggets were still imbedded in a womb of quartz, born after millenniums of existence from deep within an almost impenetrable mountain.

The Indian's dark eyes gleamed with pleasure, and the thick lips split in an evil grin. He muttered a deep grunt of approval spoken in his native Salish tongue as he fingered the nuggets.

Molly too, though tired, was pleased. At last, she would have all that her heritage and her circumstances had denied her. Store-bought biscuits in a tin, finely woven cloth for a dress, a bar of soap with the fragrance of spring violets. For those worldly goods, she had followed this man deep into the wilderness, traveling for days through almost impossible terrain, until there was no longer the slightest trace of civilization. He was old, at least compared to her own adolescence, but still tall and handsome. And as she had observed, Slumach possessed an almost uncanny familiarity with this vast wilderness that no doubt had been responsible for their very survival.

15

It no longer mattered about the guarded whispers, the rumors, the diverted glances that had surrounded Slumach the Indian. Nor had she heeded the urgent warnings and desperate pleas she received from those concerned about her safety before she left. All such worries were now far away and long forgotten.

She stood and moved closer to the fire to warm her hands and feet in the chill of the approaching night. Behind her, Slumach rose to his feet and slowly reached out his arms and turned her to face him. Though dressed like an Indian, her features bore no resemblance to his Salish tribe. Her skin was pale and translucent like that of sand, the nose and cheek bones more finely chiseled, the lips more delicately contoured.

He loosened her braids and they avalanched in a fall of jet black, waist-length hair that shimmered in the firelight. Her eyes rose to meet his, expectantly, two large pools of charcoal demurely outlined by long dark lashes that defined their almond shape. The blood of Molly's Chinese and Irish background had combined to create features that made her unusually beautiful.

Something rustled in the woods nearby. Perhaps the dry leaves in an ominous breeze was nature's foreshadowing. She turned her head to follow the sound. Something else moved—very close, very, very close. The breeze quickened suddenly, briefly, then fell, as if caught in a gasp of fright.

In the next second, the hunting knife plunged savagely into her chest and directly into her heart. She sank to the ground, and in the last seconds of life, lay there unmoving, her left arm flung from her side. Blood vomited from the wound, snaked its path along her arm to an upturned hand, where her quivering fingers pointed ironically to the gold nuggets only inches away. Then in life's closing statement, her head turned and her eyes, already dimming, shifted

16

accusingly, and came to their final rest gazing sightlessly at the gold nuggets glittering tantalizingly in the firelight.

* * *

What you have just read is merely conjecture, literary license if you like. Molly Tynan was indeed murdered. She was found floating in the Fraser River with a hunting knife still in her heart. But there was no evidence that she was murdered by Slumach, even though the hunting knife allegedly had belonged to him.

It was thought at the time that Molly was just one of eight other young women who had all followed Slumach into the wilderness. They too, had likely dreamed of a wealth that could have only belonged to a white man. All of these women, except Molly, simply disappeared.

But what of the man who they followed to their final fate? As it turns out, on the surface, he was a rather unremarkable person. John Slumach was a fifty- to sixty-year-old Indian of the Salish tribe who, so the story goes, first attracted attention in the mid-1880s when he arrived in the city of New Westminster with a pocketful of gold. Young ladies flocked to his side to share his generosity, but the rounds of saloons and visits to the brothels soon devoured his money.

And so Slumach ventured back into the wilderness north of Pitt Lake in the company of a lady of questionable character—as he would do numerous times. Two or three months later, he would reappear—alone—with a cache of gold that was soon spent on gambling, liquor, and wild women. No one was able to follow him or discover what happened to the women who didn't return.

Slumach's downfall came in a, seemingly, unrelated incident. He shot and killed a half-breed by the name of Louis

Bee, a long time acquaintance of Slumach's. The reason for the killing was never made clearer than, "bad blood."

Slumach hid from the authorities for two months before giving himself up; it was better to face the law than winter in the wilderness without provisions.

On November 15th, 1890, the jury only had to deliberate for fifteen minutes before declaring Slumach guilty. He was sentenced to hang on January 16th, 1891. Stubbornly, he admitted to committing only the one crime, and he refused to disclose the location of his mine.

On a cold, damp morning, Slumach walked to the gallows and climbed the stairs of the platform. As the hangman adjusted the noose, Slumach uttered in a whisper, "Nika memloose, mine memloose"—When I die, mine dies. Three minutes and fifty-eight seconds after the trap fell, Slumach was pronounced dead.

The words seemed harmless enough, just confirmation that Slumach had found a mine and would die protecting his secret. But generations of gold seekers have given the words the legendary status of a curse, not because of what he said, but because at least fifty-five lives have been recorded lost seeking Slumach's legendary gold mine.

Perhaps that is the nature of this curse. For if the source of Slumach's gold would die with him, then all who follow in his footsteps must, if they succeed, also die.

And one man is daring to trespass on the very legend of this curse.

His name is Jack Mould.

3
The Lust For Gold

Jack Mould is clearly a man possessed by gold.

He has devoted thirty years of his life searching for it. Specifically, his quest has been for Slumach's legendary lost gold mine. The excitement that exudes from him when the subject is mentioned will confirm that he believes the effort of the years will eventually deliver the fruits of his ambition.

Yet, his rewards to date have been meager; a small nugget here, a few ounces of gold dust there.

Exciting stuff for a weekend prospector, but hardly enough to finance half a lifetime of effort.

So what drives the man? Is he half mad? Just a little crazy? Or compelled by a burning desire to discover this legendary and elusive mine of gold?

The pursuit of gold appears to invite madness, orchestrated in bizarre and unusual ways. Wise men ponder the universe. Wealthy men indulge their whims. Hungry men dream of gold. How else does one change an existence of poverty, and strife without education or opportunity? How else does one seek one's fortune with only sheer physical effort and meager tools?

From the time when the first flakes were retrieved by man, his fascination with the mineral has been endless, drawn to the shimmering metal like a moth to a flickering flame. Gold has been witness to civilization itself. It has adorned the aristocracy, gilded cathedrals and palaces, dressed the banquet tables, masked the dead, traded as currency, and shaped the whims and indulgences of men, nations, and history. It has made poor men rich, and wealthy men poor. It's given hope to thousands and destroyed many in so doing. No other metal has so consistently been cherished throughout time and throughout the world. No other metal possesses such unique characteristics as to make it the servant of artist, craftsman, architect, and banker.

Gold can be made soft as putty, or hard as stone. It will not be destroyed by sunlight, fire, or water. It can be hammered, cut, carved, and sculpted. It will not breakdown, decompose, change in structure or in strength. It will retain its golden patina for all time. These qualities are inherent at birth.

There is no new gold. Coal or oil or gas, while they may take millions of years to form, are at least created by an ongoing process. Gold was born at the time the earth was born, conceived by the combining of gases and liquids deep within the molten womb of our planet, the child of savage geological wars. The "blood" of this battle was gold, its molten rivers running in veins, until it solidified and became entombed in quartz as the planet cooled. The never ending process of continental drift, volcanic eruption, and erosion eventually brought some gold veins to the surface. Water and wind fractured the exposed gold into nuggets and flakes, that tumbled down rushing streams to lay heavy and dead where it came to rest, sometimes in generous deposits, sometimes frugally.

In ancient times, the Egyptians mined it in the desert and panned for it along the Nile. In this highly developed, long and stable civilization, gold attained a level of artistic achievement unparalleled for a prebiblical era. And in their spiritual belief in the afterlife, the Egyptians unknowingly bequeathed to us their treasures when they buried them with their monarchy.

Mesopotamia was another ancient land that worshipped gold. The Sumerians, like the Egyptians, also buried their royalty. And in their ritual of burial, they also sacrificed humans. The death pits contain not only the grisly remains of their bodies but finely detailed jewelry, goblets, ornaments. All made of gold.

The Chinese and the Japanese both developed the art of working with gold. In India, gold became an item of personal adornment worn by those who were barely able to afford it. In Africa, gold was so plentiful at one time and in one area that it became known as the Gold Coast.

But it was religion, during the Middle Ages in Europe that gave birth to the magnificent cathedrals gleaming in gold. The renaissance emerged with gold bathing the palaces of nobility and raining upon the heads of monarchy. This lavish and extravagant use of gold would surely have bankrupted the coffers of supply. But it was not to be. Columbus not only discovered the New World but a new source of gold. And following swiftly on the heels of Columbus the plunderers of this New World gold began their conquest. The Aztec emperor Montezuma of Mexico, fell victim to the ruthless Cortez. Both his gold and his empire were seized in conquest. High in the Andean mountains, the Incas had developed a treasury of gold from vast deposits. But they too, like the Aztecs, lost both their empire and their gold to Pizarro in ruthless slaughter.

Spanish galleons returning home with tons of gold bullion, kindled a frenzy of desire throughout Europe to possess more and more. Bloodshed and death again shadowed the acquisition of gold. Men fought for, killed for, and died for gold.

It is ironic that little else, buried millions of years ago by the geology of time would move man to the heights of artistic wealth and greatness. And deliver others to the very pits of hell. For it has never been Mother Nature's intention that discovery of her gold would be accomplished without an agony of effort, despair, and death. Is there then, a curse that haunts those possessed with the fever to covet such gold? If so, is the curse intended as a warning to spare the life and soul of one more victim? Or is it just retribution for those who have trespassed into a sacred and holy world?

4

The Gold Seekers

January 24, 1848 was a day that would change the destiny of tens of thousands of men. It would ignite passion and greed in some, it would devour and destroy others. It would reach out to taunt, to tease, to entice men from every part of the world.

It was the birth of the Great American Gold Rush.

A tiny fragment of what appeared to be gold was first discovered in the stream of a sawmill about forty miles outside of Sacramento. To the owner of the mill, a Swiss named John Augustus Sutter, the implications were ominous. Far from being elated at the find, he projected the likelihood of events with trepidation.

In ten years he had acquired 50,000 acres of land, and had not only built himself an adobe house but guest houses, guard houses, storehouses, a bakery, a blacksmith, and a mill. He also successfully built and ran the industries which supported his lifestyle. He was a rancher, a farmer, a distiller, and a manager and businessman of his own empire. But the land was his only by way of a Mexican land grant. He did not hold title. And in order to maintain his empire he needed people to work for him. If gold did exist, why would one work for wages when a fortune could be at hand for the taking?

When the first few flakes of gold were subjected to a few simple tests, his fears were confirmed. Indeed it was gold, and in such plentiful quantities, that a fortune must exist in the territory.

Sutter appealed to his sawmill workers to keep the presence of gold a secret until the mill was completed and operational. At first they complied, but as more gold became visible in the millstream, the word began to spread. Soon his employees were leaving their jobs to search for gold along the banks of the American River. The news spread further and faster. Then in his annual message to Congress, President Polk referred to both the abundance and the quality of gold that had just been discovered and the word echoed around the world.

They came from South Africa, Australia, China, India, England, Ireland, Scotland, and Central and South America. Within the United States they also came from the east coast by boat, making the long, tedious, and often dangerous journey around the tip of South America to San Francisco. It was a 17,000 mile journey, five months long.

A shorter but more dangerous route was by land across the narrow girth of Panama. It shortened the sea journey by three months but took an enormous toll in human lives. Swamps and jungles, heat and rain made progress painfully slow and dangerous. Poor food and contaminated water depleted the prospective prospectors' energy and eroded their health. Dysentery, cholera, and yellow fever, diseases born out of those conditions, killed those who's health and stamina had already been compromised.

For thousands of others, the journey was made by land, from the east coast to the west coast. It was a long, arduous journey by covered wagon through mountains and deserts, across rivers and streams. Some less fortunate, traveled by horseback. Others simply walked. Wild animals and hostile Indians threatened their lives. Famine and disease claimed others. Some persevered. Some turned back. Many died along the trail, the lure of gold the perpetrator of their misfortune.

For those who survived the journey to the gold fields, a new raw land and life was to greet these "forty-niners."

They were a soup of colors and creeds. Languages, habits, religions, and politics tested the patience and acceptance of one another, the lust for gold, the only common ground they shared.

They were the rich and the poor, the young and the old, the educated and the unschooled. They were the wise and the foolish, the honest and the dishonest. They were the moral and the immoral. They were the righteous and the Christians, the sinners and the atheists. Together they prospected for gold by day. At night some chose to rest and to pray. Others sought their salvation in the saloons and the brothels.

As many as 10,000 gold seekers panned for gold in the American River or dug it from the banks along the shoreline. Not all were fortunate enough to find it. For those whose hopes ended in disappointment and despair, funds were contributed by others to see the man home again. Some, unable to accept defeat turned to menial work to support themselves. Others turned to crime. Still others simply became derelicts. Some simply disappeared.

Initially, their existence was pitiful. They were dirty and unshaven. They slept on the ground and ate what meager food could be had. Physically they drove themselves to exhaustion in the California heat. Emotionally and psychologically, they were ravaged with hope, greed, fear, jealousy, and hate. They lived for months away from their loved ones often with little or no news of them.

Law and order existed out of necessity rather than by enforcement. Without the bother of judges and juries, lynchings were deemed justifiable punishment for crimes, the nearest tree, serving as the courtroom and the gallows.

Racial discrimination, particularly against the native Indians and the Chinese was rampant. Their abusive treatment usually extended beyond what could have been considered lawful let alone humane. Gold fever brought with it the gambling, the drinking, and the dance hall girls. It was a volatile combination that often erupted in robberies, fights, and killings.

Eventually, their conditions improved. Lean-tos were put up for housing and the saloons and gambling houses were erected. When the first families joined the husbands, the churches, schools, and other amenities to this shanty-town living were added and it evolved into a community. Once the gold had been depleted some of these fledgling towns were abandoned. But for others, it made them into flourishing cities. Stocton, Sacramento, and San Francisco owe much of their early prosperity to the American Gold Rush.

In the brief ten years of the gold rush, over 500,000,000 dollars in gold was uncovered. The gold ranged from the tiniest flake to the largest nugget weighing 195 pounds. But inevitably, as the river and its banks gave up its gold, it became increasingly difficult to find. Hope faded as did the gold seekers. Camps became ghost towns. Those who had found gold made their fortunes. Some kept them. Some lost them. But the life of every man who had sought a fortune had inexorably been altered.

As for John Sutter, his once lavish empire was destroyed. The invading stampede of men trampled everything in their wake. They looted and stole what they could use, and destroyed what stood in their way. He was abandoned by his staff and left in ruin. In the years to follow, he drowned his bitterness in drink and when he died a broken, ruined man, he was destitute. That first glimmer of gold found at his sawmill had been the precursor of his destruction.

5
The Followers

The California gold rush spawned a never ending series of similar scrambles over the next fifty years. Gold strikes occurred from Alaska to Nevada, from Australia to South Africa.

In almost every case, the gold was garnered by only a few lucky men who typically had staked all the valuable claims before news of the strike ever reached the outside world.

But this did not discourage thousands of idle men who flowed north and south, east and west, seeking their fortune.

As far away as Capetown, halfway round the world, the news of the California gold rush had spread. A man named Peter Jacob Marias left for California a week after the first word of Sutter's mill. His luck was good. He established a business and though it burned down, he returned to South Africa and began prospecting in the recently discovered copper fields. He then moved to the Transvaal to prospect for gold. Within days he found indications of gold. Only a few miles away lay the Main Reef, which would soon become one of the world's richest gold deposits.

By a unique set of circumstances, only fifteen years later and having an enormous influence on the discovery of the gold deposit, on a farm at Hopetown, was the chance discovery of a 21¼ carat diamond. Diamonds were known to come from India and Brazil, not South Africa. They were also found in mica and granite which was nonexistent where the stone had been found. But more diamonds began surfacing. One 83½ carat diamond was offered for a night's shelter, by a passing goat herder. The purchaser quickly resold it for 60,000 dollars, considerably more than he had paid for it. In turn it was resold in England for 125,000 dollars. Eventually it became known as the Star of South Africa. What followed was, as could be anticipated, a diamond rush, with all the same hopes and hardships as suffered by those pursuing gold.

Despite the more favorable climate, one found dysentery, colic, and scurvy. One difference, however, was the use of the native blacks, who were hired almost as slaves to do the digging. Their diverse dialects within the languages kept them from becoming integrated and therefore were immensely more controllable. By 1895, 51,000 blacks were employed in concentration-camp confines to work the mines. Ultimately, 100 tons of diamonds have since been recovered. It made many men rich, one of them being the famous Cecil Rhodes, later associated with the De Beers Mining Company.

Meanwhile the gold seekers continued on. Some found gold, others failed. What few realized, was a patterning that would apply to all gold rushes but would be infinitely more pronounced in South Africa.

Very simply, the easy gold was found. The lone prospector would pan or pick for his gold and with luck make himself rich. But South African gold had been entombed in deep subterranean graves. Too deep for the limited individual to even begin to tap. To access gold veins at the depths they were known to be, required very sophisticated machinery and enormous manpower. Both cost money. Who had money? Those who had already made their fortune in diamonds.

Power and politics were the collateral gains beneath the fortunes. It was a gold rush for the rich and the famous. The gold, like the quartz that encased it, was a mere by-product of the pursuit. The lone gold miner was no more than an ant in an anthill until it quickly fell beneath the wheels of white supremacy and power.

Today, since Marais' discovery of those first few flecks of gold, October 7, 1853, South Africa has become recognized as the world's greatest producer of gold. The largest gold producing region within South Africa is an area thirty miles east and thirty miles west of Johannesburg, which by 1970 had produced seventy-six percent of all the gold mined in the world. The main shafts alone, of the largest of 8,785 claims belonging to the Randfontein Estates Gold Mine stretches an incredible 2,600 miles. Yet, for all the power and the glory that was attained by those few, the souls of many became the sacrificial lambs at the golden alter.

6
The Fortune Hunters

There's a land where the mountains are nameless,
And the rivers all run God knows where,
There are lives that are erring and aimless,
And deaths that just hang by a hair:
There are hardships that nobody reckons;
There are valleys unplatted and still;
There's a land—oh, it beckons and beckons,
And I want to go back—and I will.
                    Robert Service,
                    The Spell of the Yukon

Halfway back around the world, and in the northern reaches of British Columbia, something was about to unfold. Robert Henderson was a prospector after gold. For fourteen years, he had worked streams and rivers of British Columbia's north and turned up enough gold to keep alive his dream of one day finding a fortune. He was working a tributary of a river he called Gold Bottom when he turned up what appeared to be a very lucrative location. But were there other locations that might be even better?

Returning from a trading post with supplies, he met up with another prospector, George Washington Carmack. Henderson told Carmack about Gold Bottom and suggested that he work the stream and report back to him if he found gold. Having agreed to this plan Carmack, out of curiosity rather than hope, took two Indian friends and proceeded to a parallel stream called Rabbit Creek, since he had already partly explored the Gold Bottom tributary. There, lying waiting to be found was an enormous nugget! The whooping and hollering of the three men signified that they had at last struck it rich. The very next day they staked their claims. It was three weeks before Henderson learned of the discovery, and by then had become very angry at Carmack. He became even more bitter when he found so many others had already staked their claims. Eventually, due to illness, Henderson was forced to sell his claim for a mere 3,000 dollars.

That a country like Canada, so rich in natural resources, should host a gold rush of its own might well have been anticipated. Certainly to the many old-time prospectors who grubstaked their existence in the hopes of striking it rich, the presence of gold here and there kept their dreams alive. But finding the mother lode to a gold seeker was like finding the fountain of youth to someone at death's door. The Klondike gold rush, starting with that first single nugget would change the destiny of thousands of souls, some triumphantly but most often tragically.

No other gold rush in the world made the offerings as indescribably tortuous to obtain.

From August 17, 1896 when the nugget was discovered through till the following summer, word spread and gold hunters flocked to the Klondike. Having made their fortunes, the first wave of fortune hunters loaded their gold onto two steamers sailing for Seattle and San Francisco. The steamer *Excelsior* docked in San Francisco with over a ton of gold as cargo. Word spread like the plague. When the steamer, the *Portland,* docked at early dawn with over two tons of gold, she was met by a hysterically jubilant crowd of over 5,000 people. Rumor and gossip became fact. An immense fortune lay waiting somewhere north.

A massive exodus began. City police, fireman, students,

and professionals, farm laborers, businessmen, and opportunists, gamblers and thieves, filled the steamers heading north. As a result, farms, companies, and businesses were severely handicapped or bankrupted by the shortage of employees and management. Many saw the opportunities to make money by providing goods and services to the thousands in need of food, clothing, housing, transportation, supplies, and equipment. Some prepared to cater to those who had made fortunes: champagnes, wines and brandies, exotic foods, luxurious Parisian finery, bars, restaurants, casinos, gambling, drugs, prostitution. Others saw only the gold.

Most were ignorant of where they were going or how they were to get there. Some believed they could travel by road, by train, even by bicycle as if it were to be nothing more than a day's journey. Over a million people made plans to travel to the Klondike. Less than 100,000 made it. Some barely survived the first leg of the journey up the coast to the Alaska panhandle. Between Skagway and Juneau, sixty-five people lost their lives when a ship that carried dynamite exploded. Little did they know that their treacherous trip by sea was only the beginning of a journey into the pit of hell.

They arrived at Dyea Inlet on the Alaska coast. Now they must make the trek upriver through the coast mountains to Dawson in the Yukon. They faced, as their first option, the grueling thirty-five mile Chilkoot Trail. In good weather it was passable but too high for pack animals to negotiate. The second route at a lower elevation and therefore suitable for pack animals was the White Trail, beginning at Skagway, though it was forty-five miles long.

Perhaps the town of Skagway might have foreshadowed what lay ahead of these, for the most part, neophytes.

It was a town ruled by a corrupt and unconscionable con man, Jefferson (Soapy) Smith. His sole and primary purpose was to divert dollars from the men into his own coffers. He watered down whiskey and stacked the decks of both the cards and every other gambling game. He operated phony commercial businesses like freight companies, ticket offices, brokerage firms, and telegraph offices, all with his own specially trained con men to run them. Murder was a convenient way of resolving any complaints or objections to his business dealings. The nights in Skagway shrieked of barroom brawls, seductive catcalls of prostitutes, cries in the night for help, and gun shots, all heard against the tinkling of pianos and laughter from the diners, saloons, and brothels that lined the streets.

This then was a departure point. And from such a hell-hole they ventured into a world far, far worse.

The Canadian authorities through the jurisdiction of the Royal Canadian Mounted Police had, in an effort to ensure these hopefuls a better chance of surviving their trip and their time into the Klondike, imposed a mandatory require-ment for each man, of one full-year's supply of food, and essential equipment. They established a post for inspection at the top of the pass and each man's supplies were sub-jected to review. Single file, a human chain of bent and straining men, persevered to climb up a forty-five degree mountain, to a 3,000-foot summit carrying at best, a mere fifty-pound pack. It required fifty, six-hour treks often in freezing blizzards in many feet of snow to meet the required quota. Even with advances in dehydration and evaporation of food, a year's supply equated to one ton, for one man.

Most lived, some died. Some suffered snow blindness, some hypothermia. Some died by avalanche, and some by suicide. In April of 1898, an avalanche took more than sixty lives. Adding to the indignity of an untimely death by these hopefuls, Soapy Smith became coroner, in order to relieve the bodies of any possible collateral.

An estimated 22,000 men, persevered in desperation,

fear and hope, to the top, with their provisions, so they could continue their journey to their promised land. To add salt to their wounds, along with the RCMP inspection post, they also encountered a customs house, and those with American outfits, were required to pay duty (in total 150,000 dollars) as they crossed the divide into Canada.

Having made the summit, passed inspection, and paid duties, there remained a relatively easy journey to the shores of Lake Linderman.

In the meantime, those on the White Pass route were having their own difficulties.

Initially, they packed their supplies on horses, as they began their journey through swampland. After that though, it became a murderous, twisting, two-foot wide path, leading to a 2,000-foot climb, with sinkholes simply devouring horses, packs, and often their owners. Two more mountains had yet to be transgressed. Unbelievably cruel to both man and creature, at least 5,000 horses were lost, causing one chasm, because of the smell of rotting horse flesh, to be named Dead Horse Gulch.

Once over the Chilkoot Pass and the White Pass, the routes merged into one, forming a mass of humanity. Thirty-five-thousand men lined the banks of a river for over sixty-five miles as they fervently bent to the task of building a boat that would take them down the river through rapids, canyons, and waterfalls. They built every conceivable kind of boat that would float. From sternwheelers, to canoes, dinghies to dug-outs. Again, through failure and sustained effort to try again, most made it. Others, many others, were lost along the way.

With either pass and then the water route to contend with, the conditions were unbelievably grueling. They suffered from snow blindness, cold, fatigue, exhaustion, loneliness, fear. They would die by freezing to death, falls, avalanches, blizzards, suicide, and murder. They would lose their way and then their lives, starve to death or drown. No other gold rush subjected men to such unbearable odds for the reward it so tantalizingly offered.

While so many continued to eke their way into the Klondike, those who arrived first were now desperate to leave. Those who were successful and those who had failed, had had enough. And beneath their desperate desire to get out was an even more life threatening reason to leave. The lack of food supplies was bringing them to the brink of starvation. So many men, so remote a location, and so arduous was the route, that supplies could not be maintained. Coupled with the bitter, often fifty-below temperatures, the fatigue, dysentery, scurvy, and respiratory illnesses they suffered, malnutrition now threatened to kill them off in masses. Their way out was even more arduous than their way in. It was indeed a godforsaken land. And it must have seemed to the early prospectors who had been for months without a single word of news from family or the outside world, that they indeed had been forgotten and erased from the very face of the earth.

But despite the nightmare they endured, a fortune in gold was recovered. The peak year of 1890 saw 22,000,000 dollars recovered. In all, over a 100,000,000 dollars was recovered from the Dawson area in the Yukon. But for many, particularly after the first few months of the strike, the easy gold had gone, and many worked long and hard before striking it rich. Others never did. When word of a strike at Nome, Alaska, was rumored, those in despair and those with eternal hope, fled the Yukon to pursue another dream. And so history bears silent witness to the lust in the heart of man that burns eternally for this rare and precious metal, that continues to lure man in its endless pursuit.

7
A Pox On Ye

I put the book down on top of my other research material and turned out the light. It was a cold and lonely night. The wind rattled at the windows and the rain beat down in unending misery. The last flowers of fall had crumbled in the rain, the birds sat silently in the trees, and the moon sulked behind forbidding clouds. It was as if the world had gone into mourning.

My thoughts drifted back to a recent interview with Jack Mould.

The subject had been Slumach's curse, and I had questioned him skeptically on the curse, it's origin, and nature.

"Tell me about Slumach's curse, Jack. Do you believe in it?"

"Mostly not," he replied vaguely.

"Mostly when, then?" I answered, with roughly equal terseness.

"When I'm alone on the mountain. I think about it sometimes. 'Specially after I've drunk the last beer. It's a curse in itself to be alone on that mountain with no beer," he teased.

"So you don't believe in the curse, then?"

"There might be a curse. Who knows? My dad believed in it. I haven't given it too much thought. Doin' that would've stopped me lookin' for the gold, wouldn't it?" he added defensively. "But there's some that believe. And many a dead man who mighta wished he had," he ended ominously.

My meeting with Jack had left a peculiar mood in my mind. As if I had somehow been touched—or tainted by this unknown world. Several hours of reading later, the mood was even more pervasive. I had been an agnostic as far as curses were concerned. In those dark hours of night I stood on the threshold of belief.

Curses have appeared in history from the beginning of man to the present day. The Bible is rampant with them. Magistrates and priests in Greek times used curses to ward off enemies of the state and offenders of the law. The Christian ritual of excommunication from the church is in essence a curse, designed to remove from the sight of God those who had sinned. The bell, book, and candle, which it is known as, is symbolically performed by the cleric reading the curse from a book which is then closed, a bell rung, as if tolled for the dead, and a candle extinguished, removing the sinner's image from God. Curses have been used on graves to protect them from plunders as we've already seen. This practice was used in the ancient world as well as Asia and northern Europe. Even Shakespeare chose a curse as an epitaph for his tombstone. It reads:

Good friend, for Jesu's sake forbear,
To dig the dust enclosed here.
Blest be the man that spares these stones,
And curst be he that moves my bones.

Sinister as they may sound, not all curses were meant to cause harm. For the most, curses were used as a simple and effective way of maintaining law and order and to ensure appropriate behavior in the prescribed social structure of a community, religion, tribe, or custom.

Various methods were used to dispense the curse. Powders and herbs, chants, effigies, cursing the hair or fingernails of the wrongdoer are all effective methods. An unusual form of inflicting a curse among the Aborigines of Australia was "bone pointing." The bone may indeed be bone, (that of the kangaroo, emu, or human) stone, or wood with a braid of hair attached at one end. The hunters stalk their victim and when found, the bone is pointed at the victim and he is cursed. Well documented cases exist of healthy, able-bodied men—who despite exhaustive medical examinations that include X-rays, spinal taps, blood tests, and urinalysis, have died, days after being boned.

When in fact there is no physical contact, no induced drugs, poisons, injections, or potions, how does a healthy individual who has been cursed, suddenly die? The finality of death prevents any possibility of it being dismissed as a hoax, a magician's trick, or the mere mumbo jumbo of black magic and witchcraft. Nor can it be pigeonholed as something out of the medieval ages, locked away in the coffin of history.

As recently as 1946, and ironically on a Friday the thirteenth, a midwife was called to deliver three infants. Mysteriously and cruelly, she placed a curse on each of the baby girls. In her evil prophecy, she condemned one to die before the age of sixteen, another to die before the age of twenty-one, and the third to die before the age of twenty-three.

Fifteen years later, the first girl was involved in a car accident and died. The second girl, on the eve of her twenty-first birthday was killed by gunfire in a nightclub shooting. The third girl was admitted to a Baltimore hospital for observation when she proclaimed that she too was destined to die. Doctors could find absolutely nothing wrong with her. Yet two days before her twenty-third birthday, she was discovered in her hospital bed, dead.

While the physical cause of death by a curse may be unexplainable, the psychological reasons are much more evident. For a curse to hold the power of its intention, the victim must be a believer, as must the person inflicting the curse. The society in which they live must also believe as they do. When all the believers are absolute, the result is for all intents and purposes, ordained. When one is cursed, and therefore ostracized from a society where they are looked upon as nonexistent, already dead, living becomes supremely more difficult than dying. It is believed that the mind controls simply override the mechanical systems of the body, and a switch is turned to off.

Oversimplification perhaps. But it is after all, the mind that remains for science, one of the last frontiers of discovery.

Slumach approached the gallows with stoic resignation. It had been a quick verdict and an equally speedy sentence. There would be no appeals, no lengthy stays on death row. He was an Indian and he was condemned to die by hanging. He had been sentenced to hang for the murder of one man. There were those who believed him to be guilty of the murder of several more.

His hands secured behind his back, his eyes blindfolded, he stood while being blessed by the words of Father Morgan, the final farewell that would deliver him from life through death, and back to his spirit world.

Moments before the executioner made his move, Slumach uttered his famed curse in a low guttural voice. It remained to haunt the lives of so many men, who died strangely and mysteriously, following in the footsteps of the man on the gallows. Fate? Prediction? Or curse?

8
Curse of the White Man

Historically, both man-made and natural disasters have by many, been viewed as curses, a pox upon a country, a population, a civilization. The Great Flood, the Bubonic Plague, the extermination of the Jews, and most wars, First, Second, Korean, Vietnam, Iraq. To the Indians of British Columbia, perhaps the greatest curse of all came to them unknowingly, disguised in a new and unfamiliar form.

The white man.

The arrival of first the explorers and then the settlers was met with a brew of fear, curiosity, expectation, and superstition.

The white man was a strange creature indeed. He spoke a different language, used strange materials, cloaked himself in peculiar clothes, and expressed a keen interest in his trading. Intrigued by this new and different breed of man, the Indians contemplated just what dividends might come their way.

It was a multifaceted spectrum though. There were tribes that were hostile to the white man and tribes hostile to each other. There were tribes friendly to each other, and friendly also to the white man.

In the unpredictable winds of friends and foes, the white man built his forts and his bastions and guarded his tiny colonies with muskets and canons.

Suddenly, it changed.

Gold was discovered on the Fraser River. The year was 1858.

Within months, thousands of prospectors, tradesmen, suppliers, and shopkeepers flooded to the Lower Mainland, principally Victoria on Vancouver Island and New Westminster on the mainland, seeking the opportunity to participate in the prosperity. Two years later, an even richer gold field was discovered in the Cariboo. A prominent Englishmen, Alfred Waddington proposed a road from the Cariboo to Bute Inlet to better facilitate the transportation to and from the gold fields.

The natives were caught in the confusion of cultures: theirs familiar, traditional—the white man's, new, strange. Some stayed with their heritage, some adopted the white man's world. Others, lost in the maze turned corrupt, apathetic, immoral, their values and their culture confused. Some quickly became an undesirable blend of nuisance, annoyance, and trouble. Firearms and alcohol, unknown before the white man, now flamed the fires between the Indians and the whites and amongst themselves.

Then a solitary man arrived in Victoria from San Francisco. Unknowingly, he would be responsible for turning the tide of devastation for the Indians and ultimately, almost erase a culture that was reaching its zenith.

He carried the deadly disease smallpox.

All too aware of the potential threat of an epidemic, authorities urged the public to go to their doctors for vaccination. To contain the spread of the disease, isolation was recommended and then enforced for those who had become infected. The natives with less than acceptable living conditions, were some of the first to die.

Many Indians worked in family homes as maids, in restaurants and hotels while others unemployed, camped in huts sprinkled throughout the city and on the beaches. Alarmed at the danger this posed, the natives were told to leave

Victoria. Some left willingly. Others who protested, had their huts burned to the ground. With little option, they returned to their villages, taking the deadly disease with them.

The result was tragic. Isolated in remote villages along the coast and inland, without access to medical help, and ignorant of how the disease was transmitted, smallpox spread rapidly, through the naive handling of clothing, housing, and the burial of bodies. July 7, the Colonist newspaper declared, "...In a few years the sight of an Indian in these parts will be considered as great a curiosity as if a mastodon were to suddenly rise from the grave which he had occupied for centuries, and claim his ancient prerogative as lord of the brute creation."

From an estimated population of 80,000 Indians, the population fell to 20,000, dwindling even further long after the epidemic had finished. Devastated by disease, and a culture destroyed by the invasion of the white man, his will and his ways, the natives would begin a long and desperate journey to rekindle their heritage that continues even today.

It was these factors compounded with others that bred the seeds of rebellion that culminated in the white man at last becoming the victim.

The Chilcotin Massacre, April, 1864.

Working on the road building project inspired by Alfred Waddington, a party of sixteen men, twelve in one group, four in another, some distance away, lay asleep in their tents in the early hours of morning. A few hundred yards away, a group of Indians camped, hired by the work party as packers. At the Homathaco River, Timothy Smith was in charge of the ferry and a large quantity of provisions and supplies needed for the road builders.

Three Indians approached Smith demanding food, and when they were refused, they shot him. With blood on their hands from killing Smith, they headed for the twelve-man work party, joined by others as they went. At early dawn they swept down over the sleeping, undefended camp, cut the tent poles, then fired indiscriminately into the collapsed tents, hacking away with their knives till all men were presumed dead. Miraculously three survived.

The second work party of four men met a similar fate. Their numbers increasing, the Indians then headed to meet a pack train carrying supplies for the road builders. Five of the eight drivers were seriously wounded, the remaining three were killed.

The fact that it was food that was taken from where the killings had occurred while money, supplies, and equipment were left behind, bears testimony to the impoverished conditions in which the Indians had been forced to live. While the road builders and others who had employed the Indians had had an abundance of food, the Indians, it's believed, were fed mere scraps. Some white men also threatened to reintroduce the dreaded disease smallpox to the Indians as a particularly cruel form of coercion. The fact that Indian women had also been abused by the white man, and the sanctity of their burial grounds had been violated added to the seeds of revenge which erupted into the massacre.

Fearing for their lives upon hearing of the massacre, white settlers fled their homesteads for safety. It was now believed that a major Indian uprising was threatening. A scouting party was formed to hunt the murderers down and avert a major outbreak of war. Bribed with gifts from the scouting party presumably on a peaceful mission, some of the murderers were persuaded to surrender and were immediately taken prisoner. Of the eight Indians captured, two became Crown witnesses, one was sentenced to imprisonment but managed to escape. Five were hanged. The rest escaped justice. It brought an end to the road building project and it severely blighted the tenuous relationships of the Indians and the white man. It is little wonder then, for those Indians who suffered at the hands of the white man, that he was indeed a creature to be cursed.

In conclusion therefore, we have peeked into the lives of countless men enraptured by visions of wealth and prosperity. We've turned the pages of history to reveal the trauma and heartbreak that has destroyed their dreams. This has been done partly to inform, but mainly to reveal that the passion for gold has a long and turbulent history. It is living history. Embracing the hopes and dreams of all those who lived and died before him, is one man whose inner soul burns with that same fire.

His name is Jack Mould.

9

Spanish Gold

Ever since Jack Mould could remember, his father always disappeared every summer for weeks on end.

Jack assumed his old man had gone fishing or trapping, because Charlie Mould always returned home from these trips with salmon aplenty and a pelt or two.

Charlie did some of that, of course, but he also went looking for gold.

From the time Charlie Mould had sat with the Indians and seen the nugget, he had been fascinated with the thought of actually finding his fortune. For almost twenty years the mountainous wilderness that stretched from Pitt Lake north to Bute Inlet had been a potent lure. Eternal hope burned brightly in his soul, but he never shared that dream with anyone, certainly not with his family, except for Jack, the son who he believed and hoped would carry his dream to fruition.

There was one winter night, like many, when his father sat in his chair by the fire, long after the family had gone to bed, nursing the embers in his pipe and staring at the flames. Jack had crept from his bed, downstairs to sit by the fire, wearing his long johns and wrapped in his mother's afghan. It was a special time between father and son. A time when his father spoke and Jack listened. Jack didn't always understand. But he listened, as if the words were somehow holy—almost like a reading from the Bible.

Patiently he waited as he always did for his father to begin.

Charlie, his pipe resting in one hand, the other in his lap spoke at last.

"They came from a land far, far away. A land rich and sophisticated and hungry for gold. They were handsome, dark men in great wooden vessels. They came to explore and search and chart new worlds, new routes. They came with knives and scissors, and razors as collateral. They came with magic: mirrors and glass and small, black beads. They spoke a strange language and looked upon the land as foreign and hostile. They viewed the primitives in their tree boats with great suspicion.

"They were in a new land, and a new sea, a maze of islands, and inlets, and channels. A point of land would appear only briefly. Then it would be devoured by fog, and at dawn remain only as a memory, uncharted, unexplored, unrecorded. What was charted was kept as a darkly guarded secret. The ship's logs and their navigational charts were vague and often erroneous testimonies to their whereabouts.

"But explorers they were and explore they did, with one purpose in mind. They looked at these strange brown men in their furs and their moccasins. They saw their fascination with a mirror. They listened to their language and their dances. And at last they saw the gold nuggets for which these people had so little use. Their hearts quickened and their dark eyes glittered. Could this land too, as had Mexico and Peru, promise a wealth of gold?

"And where might more of these nuggets be found? They followed the gaze toward the distant mountains. They followed the arrow of fingers toward one particular mountain. "

Charlie turned to look at his son.

"The Spaniards had come for gold. "

What would later become a lifetime quest for Jack, had it's first brief introduction when he was sixteen.

It was the early summer of 1954. Jack spent three weeks on his father's gill-netter. He had done this before, but one day while rooting through a chest in the wheelhouse, he discovered a gold pan. Next to it lay what was obviously prospecting equipment.

Jack waited till the evening. Ashore, by the campfire in the early night, pipe once more in hand, Charlie began the story. He began with Slumach. He told of the nugget. And he looked upward in the night sky at the mountain. Together, his father said, they would go to the mountain.

When the fire had burned itself out, Jack turned in his sleeping bag and closed his eyes. Within minutes, after days out on the open waters, he should have been asleep. Instead it was nearly dawn before sleep came at last.

Something in the night had crept inside his soul.

Some weeks later in early June, at dawn, Charlie Mould and Jack again sailed from Campbell River where the family now lived. By the close of day, they had crossed Georgia Strait, traveled up Bute Inlet, and anchored in the slough of the Cumsack River. That evening Jack caught a salmon and the two shared the meal around the campfire on shore, before returning to the boat for the night.

The next day Charlie hiked into the mountains, leaving Jack to guard the gill-netter.

Jack spent most of the morning exploring the shoreline for several miles in either direction. By the afternoon he headed inland working his way through the thick underbrush. This was a familiar world to him, one he'd known since a child. But what was entirely unfamiliar to him were some odd markings on a tree and some very old cable wire.

Charlie returned about seven in the evening, exhausted, goldless, but beaming.

In the late light of early evening, Jack hurriedly showed his father the tree and the cable.

Charlie studied both for some time before he spoke. "Well, Jack. You've found where they probably loaded the gold."

"Who loaded the gold. . . " Jack was confused.

"The Spaniards, son. And I've found where they mined it."

* * *

Spain had long neglected the Pacific Northwest. This was the last frontier in the European conquest of North America. She had been in possession of Mexico for almost three centuries, expanding north into California, Arizona, and Texas by 1700. Britain and France had shared the eastern seaboard for more than a century, although they had just engaged in a war that gave all of it to Britain.

And Russia had established colonies in Alaska early in the 1700s.

The Pacific Northwest was the last refuge of indigenous rule. The reason for this is clear. The voyage to these waters was long and difficult, requiring either a 10,000 mile journey around the notorious Cape Horn on the southern tip of South America, or an even longer voyage across the largely unexplored Pacific. Spain had a great advantage here, an advantage she squandered. From naval bases long established on the west coast of Mexico, Spanish explorers would have had a relatively easy and short voyage to the northwest coast. And when the Spaniards did eventually begin to explore the Pacific Northwest, they did so mainly to counter the southward spread of Russian Alaska, and the western expansion of Britain across what later became Canada.

The first Spanish expedition northward, under the leadership of Juan Perez, a twenty-seven-year-old navigator, was launched from the naval base in San Blas, officially to report on the level of Russian penetration, although he was also given instructions to look for metallic deposits and other valuable commodities.

Perez sailed in the *San Carlos,* along with a sister ship the *Eliza,* through Rosario Strait east of the San Juan Islands to the Georgia Strait, anchoring in what is now Bellingham Bay.

Moving slowly northward, he stopped next at Birch Bay, then Boundary Bay, and on to Point Grey. There they encountered a flotilla of dugout canoes, and traded meat, vegetables, and firewood in exchange for barrel hoops and other scraps of metal. Their journey continued on to Point Atkinson, Bowen Island, and Texada Island.

Perez then turned south, following the Vancouver Island coastline past what is now Victoria, and up the west coast to Nootka Sound, before returning back to Mexico.

Perez then made a second voyage that added no new knowledge because the single ship he commanded, being eighty-two-feet long, was too large to sail close enough to shore or into narrow inlets. This was followed by another two ship voyage commanded by Bruno Hezeta. A host of problems including storms, illness, and difficulty at sea, caused them to take four months to reach the coast of Washington state. Badly in need of fresh water and firewood, a landing party of seven men were sent ashore. Suddenly, as they attempted to beach their boat, 300 Indians sprang from the woods and savagely slaughtered them all.

Convinced that this was an ill-fated expedition, Hezeta returned to San Blas. Juan Bodega, who commanded the other ship, proceeded northward to further chart the waters. By going ashore Bodega technically claimed the territory for Spain, but because the Spaniards habitually kept their expeditions, with few exceptions, shrouded in secrecy, this claim was unknown to rival powers.

And one rival power had begun to take a keen interest in the northwest coast.

Despite the odd intrusion of foreign privateers, the vast Pacific Ocean had long been an exclusive Spanish sea. For two centuries, treasure galleons had sailed this ocean, from the Philippines to Mexico, thence to Spain, enriching the country with a fortune in spices, gold, and gems. This wealth had turned Spain into a superpower, by far the most powerful country in all of Europe throughout the 1500s and 1600s. But ever since the defeat of her mighty armada in 1588, Spain had a healthy respect for the maritime power of the island realm of Britain, and anxiously watched this naval power grow until it eclipsed that of Spain and indeed of all European powers combined.

Britain, the Spanish knew, had searched in vain for almost 200 years to find her own route to the rich Orient, a northwest passage across the top of North America that would break the Spanish monopoly of the Pacific. Every attempt had failed, so far, but British North America was a child of these groping ventures, and the child was growing rapidly. And the well-publicized first and second voyages of Captain Cook in the Pacific did little to calm Spanish fears.

On maps and charts of the 1700s, the Pacific Northwest coast was either blank, or filled with the imagined doodles of cartographers, most of whom had never been within 3,000 miles of the place. Some maps of the time showed the fabled "Anian Passage," a wide navigable waterway which connected the Pacific to Hudson Bay. This was a prize the British wanted, badly, and they set about to prove it's existence.

In 1775, the Lord Commissioners of the Admiralty appointed Captain James Cook with His Majesty's ships, the *Resolution* and the *Discovery* to undertake a third voyage and chart the unexplored Pacific Northwest. Having wintered in the newly discovered Hawaii, Cook sailed northwest, making landfall on the west coast of Vancouver Island at Nootka Sound in the spring of 1778. After a stay of one month, Cook then sailed northward, exploring far up the Alaskan coast. He sought in vain for the nonexistent Anian Passage (which at first he thought he'd found with what is now Cook Sound), but was soon forced to abandon the voyage by meeting ice and increasing cold. He returned to Hawaii, there to be murdered by native Hawaiians in February of 1779.

Cook's third and last voyage, in itself, would have been no threat to the Spanish, except for fate.

At Nootka Sound, knowing they would be headed north into cold waters, Cook's men eagerly traded with the local tribe for furs to keep them warm. The Indians wanted iron, and for that they were prepared to trade pelts of wolf, cougar, martin, raccoon, bear, wolverine, mink, weasel, and what was considered the most prized of all, the sea otter. In total, they traded 15,000 sea otter pelts for practically every nail, button, pail, and latch and all the brass on board except the navigational instruments themselves. Much later, after Cook's death, his men stopped at Macao returning home and found that these sea otter pelts, prized for their luxurious dark fur, were worth a fortune in China. News of this good fortune was eventually publicized when the journals of Cook's voyage were printed, and this led to a "sea otter fur rush" to the Pacific Northwest beginning around 1785. Dozens of British and American merchant ships began to trade along the northwest coast, leading to eventual conflict with Spain.

In May 1789, Estaban Martinez headed to Alaska with two ships under his command. Entering Nootka Sound he was met by Indians who expressed only minor interest in the metal objects he offered to trade. Worse, the Spanish saw the masts of three foreign vessels, one American and two British merchant ships anchored in the sound.

Martinez boarded these vessels, demanded they leave Spanish waters, and when the British refused, he arrested their crews and seized their ships.

This action, now called the Nootka Incident, inflamed the passions of British politicians and brought the two countries to the brink of war. Britain demanded compensation for the lost ships and insisted that the Pacific Northwest become an international zone claimed by none and open to all for trade.

Spain, no longer the superpower she had once been, reluctantly agreed to the British demands.

This agreement opened up the Pacific Northwest to free trade for some years, culminating with the dominance of the Hudson Bay Company. Spain made little attempt to compete and soon withdrew all interest in the region. Except for a liberal sprinkling of Spanish names, such as Texada, Saturna, and Galiano islands, the Spaniards left little to indicate they had ever been here.

Except for a cave, a door, and some tantalizing evidence that they had not left before mining for gold.

* * *

The cold gray light of dawn roused Charlie and Jack from the last dregs of sleep. Charlie brewed some tea while Jack gazed through the wheelhouse windows at the light drizzle that gave the morning a pervasive chill. He eyed the misty, moody tree-lined shore, wondering about what his father had told him last night, and the planned day's hike. Perhaps it would be wiser just to climb back into his bunk.

Charlie would have none of that, of course.

Yesterday, he had found something interesting, high up in the mountains, and he wanted to show it to Jack, hoping it would spark his son's interest in his quest. Charlie's gold fever had raged strong for almost twenty years, but he could now sense it ebbing as the years of failure kept piling up. He desperately wanted to share and pass his dream to someone he could trust, and who better than his son.

After downing several mugs of hot tea, Charlie was ready to go, but it took a curse or two to get Jack fully dressed and mobile.

"Dad, I think its crazy to leave this boat, all alone, for an entire day. What if someone comes along, and steals it. "

"It's my bloody boat. I'm willing to chance it," came the terse reply. "C'mon, lets get going. It's almost eight. " Charlie checked the anchor was set, then together he and Jack clambered into the small dinghy and rowed the thirty yards to shore. They dragged the dinghy into the undergrowth, and set off, up a rough but discernable path into the forest. At least the drizzle had stopped. For two hours, they clambered upwards. Now that they were committed, Jack's early reluctance vanished with the mist that they gradually climbed above.

The morning sun cheered his mood. He led the way, urging his father onward, joking and laughing, gradually beginning to appreciate the rugged beauty of this wilderness.

They paused to rest.

Charlie poured them a mug of tea from a thermos, while they nibbled on biscuits, and gazed at Bute Inlet far below.

Jack searched in vain for their boat, but from their vantage point it was not to be seen.

They moved on, into terrain ever more rugged and dangerous. The trail, such as it was, now led along the edge of a precipice, then up the rocky bank of a tumbling creek, then past a boulder strewn area undoubtedly the retch of an avalanche or landslide, ever upward. They were high up the mountain, but had no idea how high.

To Jack, the ridge of peaks ahead, if that was their goal, seemed as remote as ever.

Around noon, after a trek of four hours with just one ten-minute rest, they paused for lunch by the grassy bank of yet another creek.

Charlie gobbled down his biscuits and tea, then unpacked his gold pan and dipped it into the water. As always, the water was bitterly cold. Understandable, because this creek was just a short rush from the icy peaks that crested the mountain.

Jack assumed this was just a convenient stop, but when he urged his father to pack up, Charlie nodded toward a red scarf, which he had tied to the tree the previous day. "We're almost there, Jack. " He pointed at the small glimmers of gold shining in his pan. "

"Is that really gold?"

"Yes, but it's worth only a few dollars. " Charlie looked from the gold pan up to his son. Excitement glittered in his eyes. "But it's a sign. . . it could mean a fortune. "

He cast the gold pan aside and stood. "Come, I've got something to show you. Follow me. "

Charlie crossed the creek, stepping spritely on a boulder midstream, and disappeared into the trees.

Jack followed him for about 200 yards and emerged into a small clearing against a steep rock face where his father stood gazing into the dark gaping hole of a large cave.

Charlie unpacked a flashlight, and led the way inside.

Jack felt the dank, cloying darkness ooze around them like molasses, and moved closer to his father and his comforting beam of light.

He couldn't tell how high the cave was, just that it was high enough to stand erect, and it seemed to go into the mountain some ways.

Charlie paused and swept the flashlight over the walls of the cave. "See that, Jack?"

"What?" Jack had no idea what his father meant.

"Look at the walls. That's not the wall formation of a

natural cave. Something's been done to them. Look, there, see those large scallop shaped areas?

"Someone shaped them.

"This cave is man-made, or at the very least, its a natural cave that's been enlarged by human hands. "

Jack gazed at the walls.

They did seem unnaturally smooth, not at all like the caves he had explored as a young boy. "Yeah, I see what you mean, dad. But who would dig a cave. way up here?"

"Good question, son. I asked myself the same question yesterday. Someone went to a lot of trouble here.

"I think that someone was looking for gold. And I'm hoping they didn't find it, not all of it anyway. C'mon, I've got somethin' else to show you, outside. "

They emerged from the cave and moved a few yards along the rock face of the steep cliff that towered several hundred feet above them. Charlie stooped to examine the ground and pointed to a large pile of charred, almost fossilized wood. To Jack, it looked like the remains of a large campfire, but Charlie set him right.

"Nope, its more than that, Jack. I've done some reading on old mining methods.

"In the old days, it was no easy matter to dig a hole in solid rock like this. But they improvised.

"First they would build a framework of timbers along the rock face and then light a fire at the base to get them ignited. When as much heat as possible from the fire had been absorbed by the rock, they quickly threw cold water on the rock striking it at the same time with picks and hammers. Great scallop shaped portions of rock would break away. By repeating the exercise, they were able to tunnel deep into the rock. That's what I figure those charred timbers are. "

"Geez, that's clever. So who did it? Indians?"

"No, I'm pretty sure it was Spaniards. "

"Spaniards? Here?"

"Probably. C'mon, I've got something else to show you."

Charlie led Jack into a nearby pocket of thick underbrush, and pointed down at a rotting slab of mossy wood.

"See that?"

Jack stared down at it. "Looks like an old carved door to me," replied Jack.

"That's what it is, lad. That's what it is. It's a cedar door, but look at the carving."

Charlie scraped and peeled some moss away. "Those figures, see 'em? They show the kinds of armor and helmets worn by Spanish soldiers."

Jack stared at the door. The images Charlie had revealed, worn almost smooth, did indeed look like soldiers, at least they did now, once his dad had pointed them out.

But Spanish soldiers? Well, Jack wasn't sure about that, but if his father said they were Spanish, they were probably Spanish.

"Geez, that's interesting. A Spanish door, here, high up in the mountains of B. C. How do you suppose it got here?"

"Good question. I didn't say, by the way, that it was a Spanish door. It might well be the work of some Indian craftsman.

"Our coast Indians were masters at working with cedar, you know. I'm sure you know all about their totem poles and the like, and they often had carved doors on their longhouses.

"Anyway, the point is, the door might be Spanish-made, or it might be Indian-made, but the images they show are Spanish soldiers, and that means, of course, that the Spanish were here, or near here.

"If the Indians carved that door, they copied what they'd obviously seen."

"Yeah, I'd have to agree with that," replied Jack logically. "How else would they know about Spaniards?"

"There's more. Jack. Lots more. "

With considerable effort, Charlie retrieved from the bushes an enormous bucket. The iron framework of two intersecting half circles bore the last rotting shreds of the leather that lined it. Inside the bucket were two grooved metal wheels, the remains of a pulley block and tackle rig.

"One things for sure lad, that's no Indian bucket.

"I think we can be fairly sure the Spanish were here.

"Right here in this spot. And I think they dug that cave, and the only reason they'd do that was to mine for gold. They were damned fond of gold. Remember the markings you found on the trees, down by the beach, yesterday?"

"Sure. . . "

"Well, that's what I meant when I said you'd found where they loaded the gold, and I found where they mined it.

"I'm not sure they did find gold, mind you, but there's gold in the creeks around here, not a lot, but some.

"And somebody went to a hell of a lot of trouble digging that cave. I figure a few dozen men spent a year or two doing that work. So either they were bloody fools, or they were on to something. "

"So you're sayin' that this is an old Spanish gold mine? And now that we've found it, we're rich?" His boyish excitement could hardly be contained.

Charlie laughed.

"Maybe, Jack. I've trekked high and low over these mountains, every summer, for twenty years. " He looked at his son. "That's longer than you've been alive. Anyway, I keep finding tantalizing bits of evidence that there's gold in these mountains, but I've not found enough of it yet to get too excited about.

"The cave looks barren to me, but you'd expect that. The Spanish would never have left if they'd found the mother lode I'm after. "

For a moment there was silence. Then Charlie seemed to sense the need to leave.

"C'mon, son, we'd better be heading back to our boat. It's getting late. We'll come back and give this place a good search, tomorrow. "

"Tomorrow! You're kidding. Right?"

"Nope. "

"You can't be serious, dad. It's a four-hour hike, each way. I'd rather camp out here, in the cave. "

"We can't leave the boat by itself all night. A few hours during the day, is one thing, but a whole night? Someone will steal it for sure. C'mon let's go. It's four hours up, but only three hours down. Remember, I did this yesterday while you were beachcombing. If I can do it twice, so can you. "

Mumbling and grumbling, Jack followed Charlie back down the mountain, and although the pace was faster, it made it even more dangerous than the climb up.

One mile from the boat, Charlie slipped on some slimy fungi, badly twisting his ankle, and rolled for about twenty yards downhill, bruising most of his body.

Jack half carried his father back to the shore, then into the dinghy, and back aboard the boat. They had no choice but to head for home the next morning.

Weeks passed before his father's ankle had healed enough for him to walk. Even then he limped, often wincing when an awkward or unanticipated weight was placed on his foot.

Jack and Charlie never did get back to the Spanish cave.

Fate intervened, for a wife, not gold, soon filled Jack's mind.

It would be many years before the call of the gold would bring him back to Charlie's mountain.

But what of the Spanish? Did they really find gold in British Columbia? Jack has no doubt.

For him, the evidence he saw with his own eyes is too compelling. In the naval archives in Madrid, a page in a book of history speaks of the gold that came from the longest channel going into the continent across from Quadra Island.

That channel is Bute Inlet. And at the tip of Bute Inlet is a mountain.

A mountain that someday he would call his own.

Jack's mountain.

10
A Trapper's Tale

The night, bathed in an early frost, glistened under the eye of a full moon. In a small clearing by the stream, three men huddled cross-legged under blankets. A fourth man sat a small distance apart, leaned against a fallen log, and observed the others. His store-bought shirt and leather jacket were pulled up around his neck to fend off the cold. The log sheltered and protected his back, offering him some, if slight, security.

His primary defense, however, came from the loaded Winchester by his side.

He considered a rifle an essential tool of self-preservation in the desolate reaches of Bute Inlet where bear and cougar roamed. Under the immense Douglas firs surrounding the men, the horses stood at rest, their heads lowered, their eyes closed. Only the hooting of an owl, or the scurryings of other nocturnal creatures roused them from their rest. They had long since accepted the deep guttural tones of the men, the occasional raised voice, the quick ripple of laughter, and later the silence.

The man resting against the log was tired. It had been a long day and dawn would come only too soon. He stirred the tobacco in his pipe and glanced over at the spoils for the day, one lynx, one deer, three mink, and a fox, their hides and pelts already cleaned and salted to preserve them till trading time.

The whiskey bottle made the rounds once again among the three other men, already mellow with liquor. The flames of the campfire flickered across the bronze skin of their broad flat faces, and glinted on their long, dark hair and deep brown eyes. In contrast, the man leaning against the log had remained sober, his blue eyes alert and responsive. The camaraderie of the evening was, like many other evenings, largely circumstantial, made so by the nature and purpose of their existence. A trapline in the wilderness, the need to survive against the ever present threat of accident, injury, or death.

The conversation of the three Indians had become animated, punctuated by boastful exaggerations and gestures. The liquor had oiled their tongues and eroded their inhibitions. Caution and discretion rose and floated away like the smoke from the campfire. One of the men reached for a pouch at his waist and extracted an object, heralding it in the palm of his hand high in the air, to the inebrious laughter and shouts of the others. He boastfully rose to his feet and drunkenly staggered over to the man by the log.

Into the man's hand, he dropped an enormous gold nugget. It lay heavy, rich, and proud of its mineral content. Slowly, the man measured the weight of the nugget in his hand, feeling the cold crisp edges, beginning to imagine how many more their might be. The question was never spoken. But it was understood. The Indian slowly turned his head, and his eyes moved upwards. Then unsteadily he raised his hand and pointed to the top of a nearby mountain that dominated their world.

For a moment there was utter silence, as though a spell had descended upon them all. Then an unusually cold breeze swept down from the mountain. In response, the man retrieved the nugget and staggered back to the others.

The talk and laughter began to peter out as the whiskey bottle now lay empty.

61

The fire died down to glowing embers. Shortly, the three men were asleep.

An hour passed. Then stealthily the man by the log arose and retrieved his pelts. Silently he crept to his horse, packed his pelts and rifle, mounted, and rode into the night. It was necessary. They were Indians. Friend by day, foe by night. He rode to the crest of a hill and looked back at the three mounds of still sleeping bodies, satisfied to see they had remained undisturbed. Then he turned, looking upward, and gazed long into the night at the rugged peaks of the mountain, lit by the solitary eye of a golden moon.

He was many miles away before he made camp and finally slept. And it would be many months before he would learn the fate of those he had left behind that night deep in their drunken sleep.

But the sounds of the three sleeping men were heard by another—someone who had waited the night out for precisely this moment. Someone who had listened intently to the careless words spoken in his very own dialect.

Stealthily, he parted the brush and crept slowly toward the camp. He moved very precisely, careful not to snap a twig, nor disturb a rock.

He held the hunting knife ready in his hand, his body tense, his muscles steeled. For one quick second he looked around him, then down at the men. Then he knelt suddenly, one hand over the mouth of the first victim, plunged the knife into his neck and swiftly slit his throat. Silently he moved to the second, and stabbed the knife again. There had been almost no sound, almost no movement. The third man sighed in his sleep just as the knife plunged into his throat. This time there was a small gurgle—brief, pitiful then silence. It took only a moment to retrieve the gold nugget. Then as phantomlike as he had appeared, he melted back into the night.

Charlie Mould was a long way from home. And he was

even further away from his native England. He had come to this land shortly after the Great War with the hopes and aspirations of all immigrants: to make a new life, a better life; to succeed, to prosper. Charlie was a trapper. It was a marginal life at best, full of risk and danger. For a few years in the Roaring Twenties, when furs were in demand and prices were high, he did prosper. But it was now 1932, and his adopted land lay embraced by the Great Depression.

Prices everywhere declined, especially in luxury items such as furs. Charlie's income was halved, then halved again, but he continued to trap because this was the only life he knew, and besides, it was better than shivering in the soup lines that were the lot of many of his generation. Now, as Charlie Mould stared up at the mountain in the dawn of the new day, rampant ambition coursed through his veins. He felt a sudden bond with the mountain, as if he had at last found his path to life's pinnacle.

Realistically, and he was a very realistic man, Charlie knew that his goal could not be climbed today or for many days.

It was midwinter, that's when the trapping was best but there would be deep snow at the higher elevations, impossible to traverse, and avalanches would be primed. He raised his hand in a salute, a farewell, and a promise to return. Then he turned and rode off into the mist.

* * *

The winter passed, then the spring, then a summer, fall, and another winter.

Charlie Mould had not forgotten the nugget he had held so briefly, nor the mountain he sensed had been its home.

But time has a way of passing for busy men.

Now it was October of 1934 and Charlie had come to seek his gold.

The night's final, lonely wolf call remained unanswered. Dawn crept in like a fine gray gauze to let the night slip away to rest. It was a deceptive dawn. It promised a clear crisp fall day. It brightened, enough to make a suggestion of a promise, then quickly dashed all expectations with a thick lingering layer of fog that settled on the day like the lid of a tomb. The campsite, if one could call it that—a few burning embers of a fire and a bedroll, had been cunningly chosen. A small craggy knoll obscured by trees had offered an almost 360 degree surveillance point.

A deep drop-off from a nearby cliff offered protection from the southeast, and the prevailing winds from the southwest had put him downwind of most predators.

The wolves, for all their howling and their creeping closeness, were of no concern.

They were no threat to man. As long as he was alive. And if dead, did it matter? But the cougar which stalked this desolate wilderness, could indeed be a killer. Long, lean and deadly, it prowled and pursued its quarry as cunningly and as ruthlessly as a panther in the jungle. With its notoriously small head, and a long lionlike tail, it could wait motionlessly on a tree branch to pounce. There were bears: black bears and brown bears. Although always unpredictable, they usually avoided any confrontation with man, if given a choice. In such wilderness, there was usually a choice. But there was also always the chance, if hungry or wounded or threatened, they would also kill.

And then there were the grizzlies. Powerful, fearless, the mammoth of the mountain. A man was reduced to a mere toy before the presence of a monster to become, teased, tormented, torn to shreds, or devoured, as pleased the king. Fortunately, grizzlies were rare.

This man knew about cougars and bears. He knew them well.

Charlie Mould was also a hunter.

His prey, this time, was mineral not animal. Quickly he stirred the embers into a fire for a breakfast of hardtack and tea, then he buried the coals, dispersed any signs of his presence, saddled up, and rode up a narrow path, a trail more animal than man-made.

It was treacherous. An overcast sky and swirling mist obscured the light, and this mere shadow of a trail would often pirouette suddenly into a precipice. The relief of a shallow plain would end inexplicably in a deep ravine. A knife cut no more than ten-feet wide that meant backtracking miles for another approach. Despite the conditions, Charlie slowly ascended the mountain. By late afternoon he was above 3,000 feet and, when the swirling mists allowed it, the vast and magnificent wilderness below would appear and charm his eyes. A setting sun reflected in the waters far below, heralding another dark night. A quickly chosen campsite. A small fire. Biscuits and stew. A precautionary walk before bedding down. Sleep. Unobserved, a nearby predator watched his prey. It was not a cougar, climbing the limb of a tree to leap upon its victim. Or a starving bear toying with the smell of a human as food. It was another predator, far more lethal. This time the hunter was human. This time Charlie Mould was the prey.

* * *

The night slid away to make room for the dawn. Charlie Mould stirred, stretched, then stood to test the day. The air was crisp, cold in the October morning. Winter, like an invasive cancer, was nibbling at the autumn. He would have to hurry. For he knew all to well, winter could kill.

He finished some leftover stew and biscuits for break-

65

fast, not taking the time to warm them. Then he smothered the few remaining embers of the fire, and saddled up.

He'd climbed above the dense needle-leaf forest and the vegetation had become lean and scarce. It reflected the harsh existence for survival at such a high altitude. And it would become even more difficult the further he went. Even now, his horse would occasionally lose its footing as the rock fractured and fell away, splintered by aeons of ice.

But while it marked the distance he'd traveled, it also brought home a reason for concern. He was exposed, visible, almost without cover. He could be seen from a considerable distance. Easily tracked. Easily hunted down. Now he would have to take care to ensure that he moved from cover to cover leaving only short stretches of exposure between what meager protection the trees and brush offered. It would slow him down when he was already desperate to make the best time he could. But it was necessary for survival. He knew.

Charlie was a hunter.

Just after midday, he stopped by a trickling stream to give himself and his horse a brief rest. He chewed some beef jerky, drank heavily from the stream, and refilled his canteen. Though the sun was shining, it was without warmth, like something dead inside. As it was, the days had grown shorter and shorter. Nightfall would come in a few brief hours. Time was becoming critical.

He stood and stretched the muscles in his back and shoulders then walked over to the stream. He dipped his hands in the ice-cold water and splashed his face and neck to wash away some of the grime and some of the tiredness. It was a natural, very ordinary action. At the same time something else, something that had been lurking in the back of his mind, slipped into place. An instinct. He was being hunted.

To his casual observance, there was nothing to confirm

his suspicion. No sound, no sudden movement in the brush, no glint of something foreign reflected in the sunlight. Only the whisperings of the gentle breeze rustling the trees along with the murmurings of the nearby stream.

But something, someone was there. The small hairs at the nape of his neck told him so. And the feel, the sense inside of him that he knew and trusted was too strong, for him to be wrong.

Charlie was a hunter.

Now he would have to hunt.

Once more he saddled up and continued his journey, every now and then dismounting to examine the ground. He chose denser, thicker underbrush now to bring his prey in closer to him. He traveled for over an hour, his direction shifting every so often, to make his movement unpredictable. The terrain had become even more rugged, and his detours more frequent. Someone would have to get in close to keep from losing him altogether. They would have to fully concentrate on keeping him in sight. That was what he wanted. They would be unaware of their own trail.

He let another half hour pass before he changed direction again. He was back-tracking now, returning the way he had come. This would not likely become immediately apparent to someone following him. That, he was counting on. That was why he had changed directions so many times. Then he dismounted and examined the ground where he had stopped before. There was nothing to see. He got back on his horse and rode to the next place where he had stopped before. It was there. The broken twig under the impression of the fresh footprint. A footprint that told him everything he needed to know. The footprint of a moccasin.

Charlie now knew this would be a waiting game. A deadly game. A game requiring many hours of patience and planning. He would have to posture, profile, act as though unaware, unconcerned. This was another dimension, another risk, to add to his already dangerous situation.

He had every reason to be afraid. He was entirely alone, deep in the remote and rugged wilderness. No one knew where he was because he had told no one, not even his wife, where he was really going.

He had never, in fact, told a soul about the gold or this mountain. If he failed to return and they searched for him at his usual traplines, they would not find him. They would have absolutely no reason to look for him where he was now.

But he could not afford fear. Fear made you vulnerable, made you reluctant, hesitant. He needed strength, decisiveness, timing, and above all, patience.

Why he was being hunted occupied his thoughts.

The hunter was an Indian, of that he had no doubt. Charlie knew the Indians. The Indians knew him. They respected him, he thought, for his wilderness skills. And why not. He was a skilled woodsman, far better than any other white man he knew, better than most Indians. But Charlie sensed this would not be the kind of friendly encounter he had had many times with Indian trappers; this hunter, whoever he was, had been given several opportunities to reveal his presence.

None had been taken. Charlie feared the approaching night.

He came across a small creek, the white water tumbling in a frenzy down a rock face, dashing itself into a small tumultuous pond, then ambling off in its own tiny ravine. It was a likely spot. Gold was heavy. Swept along by the rushing water, it would sink to the bottom in such a pond.

He squatted and panned several times, then moved to another spot and tried again. His movements were calculated, self-protecting. With his back to the rock face, he scanned his surroundings constantly, alert for any movement, anything untimely, unexpected. It was unlikely. It was still daylight, but he could not afford to be wrong. It would be a deadly mistake. He kept his shotgun loaded and ready beside him, just in case.

A glint of gold caught Charlie's eyes. It was nothing more than a flake, but it gleamed up at him out of the pan, enticing, tantalizing, promising more. For a split second his concentration was caught in the reflection of the gold. Was this it? Was this the place?

Then instinct returned. He cursed under his breath, chastising himself for the momentary indiscretion. It was exactly that kind of mistake he could ill afford to make. He went back to examining the gold pan, taking care to casually assess his surroundings.

For the next hour he moved slowly downstream, dipping the pan in the ice-cold water for a handful or two of gravel, and letting the water slip away as he rotated the pan back and forth and side to side. Many times the glint of gold surfaced to taunt and tease him. But they were mere shards, too small and too difficult to make the effort of retrieving them worthwhile. But they were beckoning him, taunting him with what he might find.

He took a stick and stirred the creek bottom from time to time, reaching down with his hands and picking up the gravel to examine the contents. Each time it was gravel, just that, nothing more. His hands would quickly grow stiff in the frigid water, blanching white and aching painfully. Each time he would rub some warmth and feeling into them and then plunge them back into the water.

He climbed over some rocks and panned downstream for another thirty yards to where the creek pooled in crystal-clear, icy water. Once again he stirred the bottom of the pond and then cupped his hands and scooped up some gravel. It was disappointing. He took a deep sigh and threw the gravel aside in disgust. Then he bent over the pool and repeated the same procedure. This time it was different.

Something seemed to capture his attention.

Charlie fell to his knees and pawed the creek bed.

A thunder roll of laughter erupted from deep inside his throat. He threw back his arms in a salute, and then first on one foot, and then another, danced a jig, whooping and hollering like a man gone mad. Handful after handful of rocks he examined, throwing most aside, but now and again, he kissed a rock, stashed it in his saddle bag, and resumed his search. For the next twenty minutes he continued until the last light failed him and with obvious reluctance, gave up for the night.

In the semidarkness he quickly made camp, starting a small fire with a few dry leaves and twigs. The flames warmed a can of baked beans, and with a hunk of cheese and bread, and strongly brewed tea, it constituted the evening's meal. Charlie was dog weary. He rolled out his bedroll, tended to his horse, then added more wood to the fire to provide an hour or two of smoldering warmth as he slept. The green pine gave off a lot of smoke, but Charlie liked it that way. He yawned, climbed into his bedroll, and was soon asleep.

In the dead of night, only the glowing embers of the fire marked the campsite. Slowly, stealthy, a dark figure approached the fire. His moccasined feet slipped between each twig, silently and confidently. He held a hunting knife tightly in his right hand, up against his chest, ready for the single swift action. He rounded the campfire and spotted the bedroll a few feet beyond that had been screened by the smoke. For an instant the intruder paused to secure his stance over his prey. As he raised the knife to begin its deadly ripping slash, the explosive blast of the rifle caught him full in the chest, throwing him backward to lay sprawling amidst the burning embers of the fire. The fire hissed, as if upset at this alien fuel. Then hungrily it flickered, then brightened, then settled down to consume its fleshy meal. Charlie walked out of the brush and glanced down at the bleeding and burning corpse. He rescued a leather pouch tied around the man's waist. It was heavy.

He emptied the contents into his hand and gazed down at the huge solitary nugget gleaming in the firelight. A nugget he had seen once before by the light of another campfire.

Who was this Indian? Why had he attempted murder? The Indian already had at least 2,000 dollars of gold in his possession. Robbery made no sense.

Charlie pocketed the nugget, walked over to his saddle-bags, and tossed out the useless rocks he had retrieved from the stream.

They had served their purpose well. He emptied his bedroll of the sticks and branches that had masqueraded as a sleeping body. They too, had served him well. Charlie led his horse some distance into the night. Less than a mile away, he found a suitable spot, made camp, and exhausted, crawled into his bedroll. Before sleep came he knew why he had been hunted. His would-be killer had to know this area well, had to know that Charlie's pretend gold was a fool's gold. But Charlie had obviously gotten too close to the real gold.

And the Indian did not want to share it with anyone. Certainly not with a white man.

11

Youth: Pleasure, Passion, and Pain

There were three things in life Jack hated. And two of them sat on his plate, in a miserable, cold, overcooked heap. One of them was peas and the other one was carrots. They were the bane of his existence. And it was made all the worse by his mother, a tiny, quiet, little thing, who enforcing the law laid down by his father, had seemingly dedicated her life to seeing that her son would grow up to, if not like peas and carrots, at least eat them.

He would have quite willingly sent them to the starving children in India even if he didn't know where the place was. But it seemed to him—somehow in his mother's logic, that those kids should go on starving and he should go on eating.

It wasn't really that they tasted so bad because he almost never got them in his mouth or if he did, that he ever (God forbid) had to chew or swallow them. It was just that it took so long to get them to disappear.

There he was, still sitting at the table with dinnertime long over. His brother was outside having fun and his sister was upstairs playing with her dolls and his father had retired to his chair by the fire. But his mother remained in the kitchen doing the dishes and tidying up and ever so watchfully, with clucks of encouragement every now and again, checking the progress of the despicable things.

Under this vigilance, they went by fork to his mouth where like a squirrel they were stashed either under his tongue or in the pouch of his cheek. Suitable chewing motions were carefully enacted which, with luck, seemed to relieve her concern. Then in a brief moment of his mother's inattention his hand made it to his mouth where they were quickly spit out and then jammed deep into his pocket.

It was accomplished with a great deal of fidgeting and squirming of course, which might have invited detection. But having successfully gotten the foul things into his pocket, the worst part was over. Once his plate was empty and he was at last excused from the table, he had only to get outside and feed the stuff to the dog.

Rascal apparently loved them. But Jack had once seen her lick up a whole bottle of spilled cod liver oil so, as far as Jack was concerned, she could be counted on to eat anything.

The third thing that Jack hated was short pants. This last torment was the product of his father's upbringing. Charlie Mould had been born and raised in England where the custom of dressing young boys in short pants prevailed, and the transfer to long pants became a rite of passage to adolescence around the age of twelve. Charlie Mould's son would wear short pants too, despite the incessant teasing Jack received from his schoolmates. Short pants and gum boots. Short pants at his father's insistence, gum boots out of necessity. Out behind the barn ankle deep in manure, gum boots were the uniform of a farm boy.

Jack had been born at Vancouver General Hospital April 28, 1936 and had spent his first few years in Vancouver before he, his brother Bill, his sister Helen, and his parents moved to Kelsey Bay on Vancouver Island, a small coastal community 150 miles north of Nanaimo.

It was a wholesome life for a boy. The small farm they owned provided the family with fresh eggs and milk. Berries were abundant and wild game plentiful. Unfortunately for Jack, the garden provided, along with all the other vegetables, a seemingly unending supply of peas and carrots. But the children had family pets and their own horses to ride. They had woods in which to hunt and play and streams to fish and swim.

Under the parental wand of child rearing, they were given their chores. There was always wood to chop for the kitchen stove, the jersey cow to be milked, the eggs to be collected. The barn had to be cleaned and the animals fed. There were chores in the morning and there were chores at night. In between, there was school in a one-room schoolhouse with one teacher for all ten grades.

Still there were Saturdays when school was out and there was time to play. And, as with all children, sometimes the simplest things are the most fun.

Like matches. Eddy's matches, as they were called. They were long, wooden matches and they were a daily necessity for the kitchen stoves and fireplaces in every household.

It was a Saturday and while their parents were in town to do some errands, the boys were left in the care of fourteen year old Uncle Jim. In the shed near the house, Bill and Jack had taken two of these matches, a long one and a short one. In the game they were playing, it was Jack's turn to pick. He picked the long one. That brought with it the privilege of striking the match. As he did so, the flame caught the paper lining on the walls of the shed. Before their eyes, the walls of the shed suddenly caught fire. As they made their escape the flames dug deeper into the wood and soon the entire building was ablaze. As they stood looking on aghast at the fire, the breeze now enticed the flames toward the house. Soon, without either water or nearby neighbors to lend help, the tinder-dry structure became a raging inferno. Within an hour, the house had burned to the ground. Only a few smoldering fragments remained of the family home to meet Charlie and Isabelle Mould upon their return from town.

It might well have crossed the youngster's minds that to run away and join the circus right about then might be rather timely. But solemnly they stayed to accept their punishment. Devastated by seeing only the charred remains of their home, Charlie Mould picked up his two boys, one in each arm, and with deliberate words to masquerade his bluff, dangled them threateningly over the coals.

To the boys, it was enough to make them quake in their boots. Eddy's matches henceforth were treated with a new found reverence. Fire however, many years later, would strike with uncanny rage at Jack the man, a mountain, and gold.

Childhood has its blessings. As the years slipped by, the short pants gave way to trousers. But it also had its temptations. Jack's child body began its bewildering metamorphosis into puberty. And along with it came an increasing curiosity about pretty little girls all dressed up in pretty little dresses.

Or more precisely, what was under them.

And if one was about to receive an education in what was then delicately referred to as "the birds and the bees," well, no better place to learn it than at school.

With the schoolmarm.

It seems that the schoolmarm for this one-room schoolhouse was a rather ravishing redhead, all of nineteen years old. She not only taught school in the schoolhouse but also lived there, in the one room at the back of the classroom provided as accommodation.

It wasn't long before she caught the attention of one John Warden, a logger from the nearby camp and a man twice her age. Smitten by his attention, the schoolmarm was easy prey for his romantic and sexual advances. Under the influence of the evening's several drinks which left her more than a little wobbly on her feet, she and John would make their way back to the schoolhouse. There, supposedly in private, they would consummate their relationship in wildly passionate lovemaking.

Had they not been so preoccupied, they might have noticed that they weren't quite alone. Three boys hanging onto the top of a ladder were peeking in the window, wide-eyed and fascinated. Between hushed whispers and sponta-neous sound effects, Jack, his brother Bill, and their friend Terry Graham were learning a subject not intended to be part of the curriculum of early childhood education.

It was clear that by the age of twelve, Jack was going to take on his father's build. He had grown to a height of five foot ten and a half inches, weighed in at 198 pounds and had developed heavy, well-muscled arms and shoulders. His physique however, did not exclude him from being a target for those who had to prove just how macho they really were. So he learned to fight and to fight well. Over the years justice was delivered with many broken noses and fractured jaws.

He worked the summer he turned thirteen at his first real job. But the taste of earning and spending his own money proved to be too tempting to consider giving it up to return to school. His father gave him two choices. School or work. Jack chose work. Grade seven was the end of his academic education.

Unknowingly he had just enrolled in the school of life.

Jack's teen years were typical of what most adolescents go through, namely, considerable attraction to the opposite sex. In a small town, one quickly distinguished the pretty girls from the plain girls, and of those rated most desirable, which ones were available. And if they were from out of town, one had to get to know them too. One summer day, that was what Jack and his cousin Roy set about doing, with devastating repercussions. The two fifteen-year-old girls had arrived by ferry boat from Quadra Island to spend the day in Campbell River. It was an afternoon of exploring the town and the surrounding areas, of hamburgers and cokes, jokes and laughter, fun and frolic. With a vague reference to staying overnight with relatives, the girls expressed little concern about catching the ferry back to Quadra Island. But as the time of the last ferry approached, they apparently changed their minds. In a frenzy of flight, the four teenagers arrived at the ferry quay to see the boat already pulling away. They were in Campbell River for the night, like it or not. Apparently spending the night at the relatives hadn't quite the same appeal as the alternative Jack came up with. Back to Jack's house they went and with stealthy footsteps, the four juveniles slipped into the family's holiday trailer parked in the backyard. Along with the kids went a bottle of rye whiskey. This, the boys had acquired along the way, with less than honorable intentions in their heads and, likely, other parts of their anatomy. But three glasses to Jack, unfortunately, was his undoing. Worldly wise with the wisdom of his seventeen years he had contemplated a night of never ending passion. But he had not counted on the rye.

Sun, fu,n and the whiskey despite his most ardent thoughts, did him in. He woke startled and disappointed the morning after to find he had slept the night away. The girls by now were suffering the pangs of guilt as a result of their irresponsibility, and it was imperative that they leave the trailer before they were discovered. Two hours later, leaving the local coffee shop, they were stopped by the RCMP and questioned. When the girls' identity was verified they were taken to the police station. Soon after, the enraged parents arrived to take their erring daughters home. But the law would not be as lenient on the boys.

Ultimately, Jack was charged and sentenced to nine months at the young offenders unit of Oakalla prison. Roy received six months. Jack faced his sentence with fear and anger. Prison was for criminals and he was innocent. All through his childhood he had been taught honor and fairness, right from wrong. This was unjust. But the scales of justice are not always balanced. It was the first of several hard lessons he was to learn about life. Prison has a way of making you grow up fast, hard, and wise. Jack was a formidable opponent for those who found feeble excuses for fights and strong enough that the work tasks were taken in his stride. Through his resigned endurance, the months crept by and he was released in the spring of the following year.

12
Disillusionment

Dora Lee Master was a tiny, dark, good-looking girl of fifteen, working at a nearby restaurant when Jack happened to meet her. He was eighteen-years old and only recently released from Oakalla. After those hard long months, female companionship had a decided appeal. They dated, went to dances, and did most things young couples do. They also fell in love. A year later they were married.

Somewhat prematurely, their first son Doug was born and within the following year, they had a daughter, Laura Lee. It also began to appear that Dora Lee, not much more than a child herself was finding the responsibilities of being a wife and a mother burdensome. The good times had gone. And so had Jack, for ten days at a time, working as a high rigger for a logging company.

Soon the rumors began to reach Jack on his return that Dora Lee had started finding her own entertainment. Word of all-night parties and the boyfriends to share the fun began to circulate. He returned one time to find her living it up at the local legion. Afraid of what Jack might do to the place when he found her, the manager sympathetically but protectively denied him entry.

In through the back door he went like a raging bull and soon the place was in shambles. Restitution eventually resolved the matter. Angry, humiliated, embarrassed, and disappointed with his wife and his marriage, he nevertheless persevered, each time hoping on his return things would be different.

If they were different, it was because they'd gotten worse. Back from camp again early one morning, a neighbor informed him that Jack Innes, Jack's boss who owned his own logging company and was considered by Jack a friend, had spent the night at the house. Confronting his wife, Jack asked her, "did Jack Innes spend the night here?"

"Yes," she replied quite innocently. "He slept in Dougie's bed." At the time the youngster was going through a bed wetting problem. Habitually, each night he'd wet his bed. Jack went into his son's bedroom and pulled down the covers. Predictably, the sheets were sodden with urine. He looked her directly in the eye and asked her, "and he slept in that?"

Despite the overwhelming proof of her infidelity, he remained in the deteriorating marriage. Then several months later he came back to town, stopping to buy groceries to bring home. This time he was informed there had been a party at the house the previous evening. Overheard outside on the front lawn, a group of guys had been arguing about who was going to take Dora Lee to bed first. This was the last and final blow. Jack had had enough. In the kitchen and in front of Dora Lee, he emptied the contents of the milk bottles on the floor and threw the groceries after the milk.

"I'll be damned if I'm going to feed you and your friends. As far as I'm concerned the party's over!" He stormed into the bedroom and packed his bags, threw them in the car and drove off. For several hours he drove around trying to cool down, overcome his anger, and make some sense out of his life. But even the car seemed to remind him of her infidelity. He'd been humiliated to learn that it had been a frequent if brief convenience for her encounters.

Finally in an act to emotionally sever the relationship,

he drove to the ramp of the wharf and parked the car. He took his suitcases from the trunk then put the car in gear. Slowly the car crept ahead onto to the wharf then toppled over the edge into the sea.

The ripples of water marked the grave of the vehicle and the marriage.

13
Search and Rescue

Back in Campbell River, Jack renewed an old time friendship with John Humphries, Captain of the *Humphrey J.,* the vessel assigned to the Air, Sea and Rescue station in Comox. Jack and John had done a lot of fishing for steelhead together over the years, and John, ten years older than Jack had gained in Jack's eyes, considerable respect and admiration.

Not surprisingly, Jack became a volunteer. There seemed little in life that intimidated him: man, beast, or nature. Despite having run aground of the law, his basic good samaritan upbringing had not been tarnished. He had never considered himself a hero, ever. But if he could help someone in distress, possibly save a life or lives, or deal with the particularly gruesome aspects of death in order to resolve a murder, suicide, or fatal accident, he was all too willing to help. He was a hunter, a tracker, experienced in vehicles, heavy duty equipment, and boats. All extremely useful talents in the rugged northwest. And he had seen enough blood and gore from logging, boating, and equipment accidents to send most men into a dead faint.

And while on the scene, he also had the mentality to stay calm in an emergency and a stomach that still retained his lunch under the most grisly of accident scenes.

He sat before me, as always with Pussywillow, my cat on his lap, his bear paw of a hand gently stroking her long, lustrous fur. Almost gone from memory, I urged him to recall some of the emergency calls he went on with Humphries.

"Geez, there were so many...I'd have to think."

Slowly as I prodded him into recalling some of them, the stories came—the most ghastly, horrifying, tragic circumstances to the victims involved. Most of us would never be able to blot out memories so traumatizing. For Jack, it was a part of life. He helped the living if he could. And if he couldn't, he helped the dead. Many of the names and the dates are gone but he began to sketch in the details.

"There was this guy cleanin' the deck around an open hatch of a fishing trawler. Guess he wasn't watchin' good enough and his foot slipped through the hatch and down into the gears. Took his foot off at the ankle just as clean as a whistle. Didn't have all the fancy stuff they have on them ambulances then like they do nowadays. So we did what we could to stop the bleedin' and yarded him off to the hospital. Guess somebody had to go down and get the foot out of the gear housin'—or what was left of it anyways.

"Another time we docked the *Humphrey J.* The tide is movin' with us so it's real easy. On the other side of the wharf this fishin' boat is comin' in. The guy throws us his bow line that we tie for him and then he goes to the stern that's bein' carried by the tide away from the dock. He starts the winch to pull the stern in. The distance begins to close as the coil of rope falls in a circle at his feet eh? Well, he must have been reachin' for the lever, 'cause his hand slips off the winch and out of control; the coil of rope snakes around his foot and feeds it straight into the gears. By the time I could get on board and stop the winch it had his foot almost severed, just this little bitty piece of skin keepin' it attached to his leg. Well, down I went into the galley, got a butcher knife and cut the skin holdin' it on. Seemed a lot easier movin' him that way than with his damn boot lollygaggin' off his leg. Laid him down and lit a cigarette for him.

"Funny, he was a damn good dancer before the accident. Then he got this here new foot and shoe, and damned if he wasn't just as good a dancer after."

His deep barrel-chested roar of laughter brought an end to that tale. Then he sobered.

"They weren't all accidents. Sometimes people would go missin'. I remember lots of times searchin' the mountains for hunters. What really used to piss me off is spendin' hours in the rain and the cold till near dark lookin' for someone and then find out they were home in a nice warm bed. Just hadn't bothered to tell anybody. That would really piss me off.

"And bodies. Lots of bodies. Boatin' accidents, drownin', that kind of thing. Course we didn't always find 'em."

He chuckled.

"Oh yeah, there was this one body. Been in the water a long time. Real long time. There was this RCMP guy and me. And the body was wrapped in black plastic. We had hauled it out of the water and we was attemptin' to get it to shore up the ramp of the dock. The ramp was like this...."

Jack's bear paw came up from his lap to indicate a forty-five-degree angle.

"I had the guy's arms at the wrists and I was walkin' backwards up the dock. The cop had him by the lower legs. Suddenly I got this real eerie feeling in my hands."

Despite the grisly details Jack chuckled again.

"He just startin' slippin' out of his skin. Kinda like a sausage out of its casing. Then the guy slipped right out of the plastic and landed on top of the cop and the two of them fell in a heap at the bottom of the ramp."

I don't suppose with his background, Jack was overly fond of our mounted police force by this time in his life, because the scene that he was describing he was finding highly amusing.

"Well you shoulda seen this cop. He was screamin' and strugglin' and tryin' to get this foul, rotten body off him and he was turnin' greener by the minute. He finally got to his hands and knees and then he puked his guts out. Funniest thing I think I ever did see."

This time it was a full-blown belly laugh that brought tears to his eyes. I waited till after he'd dabbed at his eyes and the laughter had subsided before I continued.

"Drownings must be particularly awful," I added tactfully.

"Yeah some are.." he agreed amicably. "Yeah, like the Quadra Island Ferry."

"Someone fell from the ferry?" I prompted.

His tone was serious now. "No, no the ferry wasn't even docked. It had left—was about fifty feet off from the wharf. One of the guys had worked the mornin' shift on the ferry and was late gettin' back on board. He had his wife and two little kids in the car. Someone I guess, had forgotten to raise the boarding ramp after the ferry had departed. It was nighttime and when he got to the end of the dock he saw all the lights of the ferry still real close and thought the ferry was still docked. Anyways, the car went right off the end of the dock into the water.

"We always kept our tanks and divin' gear ready, always used to get them filled at the hospital, cause that way we could get them filled free any time of the day or night. So when we got called, we got into our gear down at the dock and went down to search for the car. The police were givin' first aid to the parents who had somehow gotten out of the car but so far the kids hadn't been found.

"We found the car alright. Right side up and all. Dark as hell it was down there. We had safety lines between us and John managed to get a door open and he started feelin'

85

round the back seat for the kids. Then somethin' bumped his head. He reached up and there were the two kids pressed up under the roof of the car, dead."

There was a few moments of silence. I didn't ask how long and how difficult it was to recover the bodies. I didn't ask what desperate hope the parents had still clung to while Jack and John were searching for the children. And I didn't ask when the last second of hope turned to heart retching tragedy. Those were details neither of us volunteered to discuss. They, like the children, were laid to rest, unspoken.

14
Storm: The Aftermath

It was a savage night. The west coast is well known for its suddenly vicious weather. Through the testimony of history, it has become a graveyard for ships which have met their doom on the reefs and the shoals during gale and hurricane-force storms. This Friday night, April 10, 1964, might have carried a gentle spring breeze. But it did not. The seventy-five mile per hour hurricane-force winds lashed the sea to a frenzy and the waves first retreated as if to gain strength and then advanced with deadly brutality toward anything in their path. And in their path was a forty-five-foot tugboat forced onto a reef and pinioned as moment by moment the waves sought to crush the life out of the vessel. On board were two couples and their three children.

The mayday from the ship came in to the RCMP first who in turn called the Air, Sea and Rescue unit. Responding to the call, John and Jack aboard the *Humphrey J.* set out to rescue the tugboat crew. Within twenty minutes they came alongside the foundering vessel. The wind and the waves threatened their own lives as well as the crew of the tugboat. Had any one of them been washed into the sea, they would have almost instantly been lost from sight. Within minutes, the bitter forty-two-degree temperature would have condemned them to a hypothermic and useless state, with death swiftly following.

While John worked frantically at the controls to keep

his ship from collision and yet maintain closeness, Jack, timing his move with the waves and the movement of the two ships, leaped aboard in a daring and dangerous jump. He caught himself by only the pipe railing on the deck. But there was precious little time to be thankful. Time itself was running out. The boat lurched sickeningly under the battering of each crushing wave and teetered on the brink of capsizing.

Without ceremony, he seized the first child and when the exact moment came when the two ships reared together, hurled both the child and himself onto the deck and then down below to safety. Then he returned for the next, timing the leap to the deck and grabbing the next child and returning the child to safety. Once again with the last child, and he had the children safely on board.

As the ship rose and plunged and the waves crashed against the hull with increasing force, he turned to the women. When they too were on board he went back for the men and they also were rescued.

The rescue had been dangerous for both Jack and John Humphries. But it had been successful. Safely back on shore the passengers generously expressed their gratitude then sought warmth and shelter. Later they proceeded to make out the required police report.

For Jack and the Captain, they had their ends to tidy up as well. But once done, tired, hungry, and thirsty, they headed for the Discovery Inn for a late night beer and steak dinner.

It was to be a decidedly untimely decision.

A few steps from the door of the Inn and in a spontaneous gesture of elation and camaraderie, Jack threw his great bear arm around John in a moment of exhilaration. Knowing that they had just saved the lives of seven people seemed at the moment a justifiable cause for exuberance.

It was a fateful coincidence. Coming out of the pub were two burly and inebriated longshoremen.

"Say, Arnie, looks like we got a coupla faggots here," one said to the other.

"Yeah," the other replied turning to face Jack. "Ain't got the guts to be a real man, eh?" The longshoreman was a giant hulk of a man, easily a head higher than Jack, but also very drunk and very intent on making trouble. Though Jack had intended to ignore the provocation, it was not that simple. Spoiling for a fight, the longshoreman made a lunge for Jack. Momentarily losing his footing as the weight of the man came down on him, Jack regained his balance, turned and brought the man down over his shoulder to a crushing blow against the pavement. Though unintentional, the man fractured his kneecap in the fall and was rendered defenseless. As Jack turned his attention now to the other man, he saw John lying unconscious on the ground as the other longshoreman continued punching him. Jack grabbed the man and with a single blow laid him on the ground. Then he hauled his buddy to his feet, got him inside and cleaned up. Though more than a little worse for wear, they proceeded to have their dinner. But it had been both an unfortunate and untimely encounter.

The next day the police charged Jack with assault causing bodily harm. There had been three witnesses to the beating. Unfortunately as character witnesses, they lacked the necessary credibility. One had already replaced the law with the Lord. Apparently he was deemed such a religious zealot, the man was disqualified from testifying.

Another was a prostitute, and the third had a criminal record as long as the proverbial arm of the law. Several other witnesses who were returning to or leaving their parked cars were in the remotest part of the parking lot offering little if any visibility to the scene. One of these was a woman who had seen next to nothing. She was told that Jack's name would be called out in the courtroom to take a seat, and therefore if she got a good look at him then, she would be able to identify him later on in the trial.

Clearly the hounds had circled the fox.

Magistrate Roderick Haig Brown sentenced Jack to two years less a day in Oakalla prison. John received a sentence of eighteen months.

The fact that these men had, over the years risked their own lives many, many times to save others, seemed to count for very little. It did however, inspire a well-intended compliment from the magistrate. After sentencing the two men, Haig Brown turned to Jack and John and, with apparent sincerity, said, "If I was ever in trouble, if I ever needed help, I would want the two of you to rescue me. I have that much confidence in your abilities."

With the sentence already passed, Jack had little to lose.

"Yeah, well you know what?" he replied. "If you was ever in trouble, I'd throw you a fuckin' boom chain."

On that final statement he was led from the courtroom.

15
Time: And Again

Life behind bars for Jack was time to be endured. If the law had been unfair in his sentencing, then so be it. Resigned to his fate, he refused all letters and visitors and committed himself to live out the duration of his time in solitary seclusion.

Out on parole two years later, Jack headed for Vancouver to make a new start in life. He had rented a house in West Vancouver and was working as a steel worker in the wave of high-rise construction that was taking place in West Vancouver and the west end of the city. Then an old friend of his, Al McKay came down from Campbell River to work in Vancouver too. The problem was, however, that Al was broke. To help him get on his feet, Jack loaned him 800 dollars. Anxious to be repaid the money he had loaned his friend, Jack willingly cooperated when Al told him about a "deal" he was working on.

The deal involved selling a number of stolen outboard motors. Apparently, the buyer for the motors had reneged. But Jack had a contact. He went to the phone book and tracked down the prospective buyer, got his address and made the call. Yes, the man was interested. A short while later Jack and Al had found the house. On the doorstep Jack met Tony Hornby, and introduced Al to Tony, then turned went back to the car and waited while they concluded their business. Arrangements had been made to send some of the motors on down to Victoria where they were to be sold. The day arrived, and the motors were on their way. En route however, they were intercepted by the RCMP. When asked who had had the motors, Jack's name was erroneously given. Al volunteered to clear Jack when they went to court. Expecting Al to keep his word, Jack remained silent about the deal and went to court confident he would be cleared. But while Jack went to court, friend Al McKay failed to appear. Abiding by the age old loyalty to a fellow friend, Jack remained silent while he was sentenced to two years in the B.C. penitentiary for possession of stolen property.

Inside the penitentiary, Jack once again resigned himself to making the best of it. He was assigned kitchen duty, one of the softer, more pleasant jobs available, though it had its moments. More than once he witnessed inmates urinating or ejaculating into the bread dough. Petty as it was, to some inmates, it gave some kind of perverse satisfaction to know that the bread was intended for consumption by the prison guards.

The guards themselves came in a variety of scruples and moralities. Some were honest, others corrupt. Some were heterosexual and some were homosexual. Some were unimpeachable and others could be manipulated, bought, or bribed.

Inmates quickly grew to know the predilections of each guard. Alcohol and drugs were available through certain ones. Cash and contraband came and went with others, to and from the outside world. Sexual "favors" were used for others. Rape, an inevitable certainty, particularly of a new inmate was frequently overlooked. And, as with the nature of men held together against their will, clashes and conflicts brewed amongst the men, and fights and stabbings were constant threats. Fortunately for Jack, he failed to ruffle the feathers of anyone spoiling for a fight. That and the fact he was a formidable opponent spared him trouble. He had friends too, like "Fats" Robinson and Tony Gardner that would have come to his aid, so he was simply left alone. But prison life breeds time to dwell on the past and stew over actual or imagined grudges.

Jack was never a "snitch." He was doing time for Al McKay. And Al Mckay in the meantime had likely crossed more people than just Jack. After he had been released from prison Jack learned of what had become of his ex-buddy Al McKay. Six months into Jack's sentence, Al McKay had been found shot to death on Granville Street. Someone had decided to deliver justice with a hand gun.

That someone was never found.

Trouble had gone out of its way to find Jack and he didn't need any more of it. He made a point to keep his record clean from that point on. Some twenty years later, he would receive his pardon. But now out on parole, he returned to Campbell River and once more picked up the pieces of his life. It wasn't long before friends and acquaintances learned he was back. And one acquaintance, in particular, decided to personally welcome him back.

Janet Robinson was a petite and very pretty twenty-two-year-old blond with a shapely figure and a vivacious personality. She and Jack had gotten to know each other casually when she had worked as a lifeguard at the neighborhood swimming pool. At the time she was married. Now divorced and the mother of five children, she called Jack to say hello. Jack arranged to meet her and renew the acquaintance. Soon they were dating on a regular basis, going to dances and parties, and enjoying the romance that quickly developed. Before long they were deeply in love.

In 1962 Jack and Janet married. Jack, who had always wanted a family, became father to year-old Richard, Denise three, Lisa five, Debra eight, and Dale ten. It was a marriage that would last twenty-four years.

16
The Quest

As a boy Jack had sat at his father's knee and listened to the tales he had been told about hunting and trapping, about boating and fishing, about animals and Indians, and ultimately, about the mountain and the gold. He'd seen the faraway look in his father's eyes, and often seen his father direct his gaze in the direction of the mountain. He had tried to imagine the dream his father had had, tried to capture the spirit of the search, tried to visualize this treasury of wealth.

To a child, it was a fantasy.

To the man, it was now the quest.

Through his early years, seeded deep within him by his father, the allure and attraction to this mysterious and elusive mine had remained alive, an ambition that someday he would fulfill. But the burden of life had been heavy and he'd had to pay his dues. But deep inside the womb of his soul, the ambition flickered and burned, growing to a fire now burning brightly.

It was time.

Even with the new responsibilities of husband, father of five, and provider for his family, the thought of the gold his father had sought was becoming foremost in his mind. Soon it would demand action.

In 1965, three years after he was married, Jack decided to attempt to trace the elusive fortune.

It came close to costing him his life.

Jack and his family had moved to Sicamous, a six-hour drive from Vancouver so that Jan could be closer to her family. Jack was working as a logging contractor at the time and he and his friend, Joe Aires, decided to borrow a boat from a friend and head off up the inlet to the foot of the mountain.

It was a disastrous trip from the start. In a rather pathetic way it had its black humor. It had it's misery. And it could as easily have had them dead.

The spring weather is at best, unpredictable—in the west coast, unforgiving. In it's violent tantrums, it lashes seas and shores unrelentlessly with wave upon wave of turbulent viciousness.

Jack and Joe were caught in the mercy of her vengeance.

The boat engine suddenly quit and stubbornly refused to restart. Offshore and drifting helplessly, they suffered the batterings of the waves while they fought quickly and expertly to correct a simple malfunction. But was it bad luck, or was it perhaps something even more mysterious, that kept two experienced men from being able to resolve the mechanical problem the engine presented.

Only by the fact that the winds were in their favor, did they find themselves, instead of drifting out to sea, being none to gently tossed ashore.

It was barely a hospitable landing. They had arrived on a narrow isolated beach drenched to the skin and shivering violently from the cold. Most of their survival gear had been either damaged or lost in trying to reach the shore. Gone were such precious items as matches, protective apparel, survival rations, emergency equipment and what little else would have made them safe or secure.

Bitterly cold, and without fire or shelter, they clung

together through the long dark hours, sleeping out of exhaustion until a cold gray dawn tore them from the night.

When the first light of day arrived, they were greeted with fog and mist. After several hours the visibility improved. Now exceedingly hungry and more than frustrated, angered and annoyed at their circumstances, they concentrated their attention on the horizon, hoping for the appearance of any passing vessel. The men searched relentlessly for any barge, tugboat, trawler or fishing boat. They had been expected to be gone for several days. There was absolutely no reason for anyone to consider them missing. An Air, Sea and Rescue search could be a week or more from being launched.

That thought alone, for the two men—well aware of what they faced—remained unspoken. Yet both knew under the conditions they were in, their survival was extremely doubtful.

The day passed into twilight and for a second night, they would sleep without food, adequate water, or shelter.

Their situation was now very serious. Alternately as their emotions swung between hope and despair, they would laugh at their predicament and then only hours later, find themselves dissolved in hopelessness and apathy. Both were too aware that lives are easily lost for the want of such simple survival items as matches, drinking water, and warm clothing.

For three nights in abject misery they endured each hour on the wind swept, desolate beach, doing all they could in the bitter west coast climate to survive. They were drenched by rain; hungry, bitterly cold, tired, weak, and facing what now seemed an almost certain death. As each day passed into another, their hope of rescue diminished. Their initial cries of laughter about their predicament faded to obtusely disguised comments about their mortality.

The morning of the fourth day appeared like all the

Old newspaper photograph of Volcanic Brown on one of his trips to town.

Human bones. More than fifty-five people have gone missing looking for the lost mine.

These bones were found near the mine. They had fallen off cliffs and were scattered by grizzly bears.

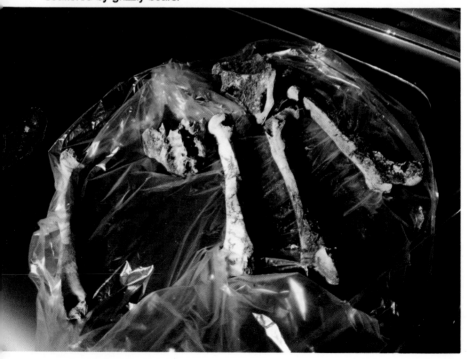

Charlie Mould, 1926, on his trapline at Bute Inlet.

Jack in front of the Southgate River, at Bute Inlet.

A picture of the old air-strip taken from the heli-port at 3,000 feet.

The creek that begins and ends nowhere!

Campsite with the swimming pool and dining room.

Jack cooking steaks on the barbecue.

Jack's brother Bill on the site.

Where the water disappears.

The three peaks.

Tent-shaped rock at Bute Inlet, May, 1989.

Jack and Jim the dowser, 1990.

Jim, ready to set dynamite.

Kelly, Jack's nephew, trenching a quartz vein.

On top of Southgate Mountain, 1989, with Bute Mountain in the background.

A spit of land on the Southgate River.

Jack and Kelly at their office on the top of Southgate Mountain. Bute Mountain is in the background.

Brother Bill at one of the Spanish caves near Bute Inlet.

Guns and power plant burned by fire when the camp was hit by lightning.

Richard, Jack's son, sitting on a 100-pound propane tank that didn't burn.

The tent-shaped rock.

Jack with the tent-shaped rock.

One of many of the creeks in the mountains around the lost mine.

others. Dank, gray, cold, and wet. Once more they emerged from a makeshift shelter to scan the horizon. Suddenly they heard the distant sounds of an as yet invisible boat through the slowly dissipating fog.

They screamed, they yelled, and though on the brink of exhaustion, they screamed again. Minutes seemed to turn to hours. Hope turned to despair. Life seemed at the moment to belong to the sea. Those on land had been abandoned, left to die like so much flotsam washed ashore by the ocean as if it was already too full to consume two more dying souls. Then as the sound of the engine wafted away and their hopes once again lay like shattered glass, the sound of the engine grew louder, and a sailboat appeared. Though the sails appeared to be catching the wind, the telltale sound of the engines signaled she was under propulsion.

Their desperately frantic shouts at last caught the attention of the sailor. Unbelievably as they watched, the boat came into view and turned in their direction. It was the answer to a prayer! Twenty minutes later the men had squared away their situation and been invited aboard.

Aboard usually means just that. Aboard the vessel. Instead Jack and Joe were invited aboard their own vessel, namely the dinghy. Grateful as they were, they climbed into the dingy, which proceeded to be towed some 100 feet behind the sailboat.

At first, rescue after three nights ashore overjoyed the men. Then slowly, their exuberance faded as the dinghy provided even less shelter than what they had had on shore. It became apparent that the owner of the boat and his paramour considered the sailboat too intimate a space to be occupied by two burly cast-offs, picked up off a deserted beach.

For an entire day and a half, they were towed behind the sailboat in the opposite direction from where they should have been headed. Colder, hungrier, and more exhausted than ever, they could only console themselves that they at least had been rescued.

Finally the sailboat docked at a tiny, remote marina. Overcome with relief at being back to civilization, they managed to dry themselves out, dig into some food, then eventually make their way home.

The trip had taken a week, and nearly cost them their lives. Once again the curse of gold had lured two men almost to their death. And again some inexplicable force had stopped Jack at a point he had not been able to trespass beyond.

For us all perhaps, certainly for Jack, it might be just as well we do not have a crystal-ball view of our future.

Jack would not know just how many times his fate would be suspended by strange and mysterious circumstances.

Unless, of course, it is the curse of Slumach. Haunting the one man who would tempt the very fury within its soul.

17
Seeds of Sorrow

Jack's life till 1986 had not been particularly charmed. He had suffered his fair share of fist fights and brawls, been attacked by both men and animals, and had witnessed many deaths, both in the logging business and in his air sea rescue days, and he endured many and often dangerous treks in the pursuit of the gold mine.

Jack could laugh and he could joke. He could listen with compassion and talk with feeling. But Jack could not and would not cry. When he was a little boy, he'd been led to believe that if you cried you were a sissy. And that was one thing Jack had stoically decided about himself. He was no sissy. But one of the most traumatic events of his life would bring him to his knees.

This time with grief.

Jack and Jan had not only shareda very good marriage but they were also friends. True, deep, and committed friends. They had raised their five children, suffered the financial ups and downs that many marriages experience, and yet kept the closeness between them alive and thriving.

The first reluctant seeds of suspicion concerning his wife Jan and a family friend by the name of Don Trask began to surface at a time when Jack was out of town much of the time, working as a logging contractor. It was early in 1987 and Jack and Jan had enjoyed a happy, comfortable relationship for nearly twenty-four years. As far as Jack believed, Jan had always been loving and faithful, a good wife, and an excellent mother. Don was a slightly built, affable fellow with charm, wit, and humor. Jan still retained the good looks and gentle, naive ways of her youth. In Jack's absence and with Don's less than honorable intentions, Jan was no match for his manipulative approaches. The relationship eventually turned into an affair.

Jack's suspicions were further aroused when he tracked Don to an out of town motel. Jan was also away, apparently visiting her folks. When Don returned, Jack invited him over. When Don walked in the door expecting the usual friendly visit, he didn't anticipate what Jack had in mind.

It wasn't a visit and it wasn't friendly. Very calmly Jack shoved the end of a shotgun into Don's mouth, pushed him down on the sofa, and suggested that Don start at the beginning and explain just what had been going on. Jan obviously alarmed at the situation, called the RCMP.

Over the next two hours, while the police attempted to get Jack to put the gun down and walk out of the house, Jack listened to, detail by detail, the events leading up to and through the affair. When at last he was satisfied with the information, he did as the police requested.

The RCMP seized the shotgun along with his other weapons, arrested him, and charged him with three counts of pointing a firearm at another individual. Only Jack knew the gun wasn't loaded. But it had been, nevertheless, a persuasive tool.

Later, the charges were dropped. The affair ended as quickly as it had begun. Within a week, Don returned to his wife. But for Jack, devastated at what he had learned, his marriage was over. The trust he had all through the years for his wife had been eroded. Normally forgiving by nature, he could not bring himself to renew his faith in her. Despite her pleas and her apologizes, there was no turning back.

First days, then weeks, and finally months slipped by. He could not rekindle his faith in Jan.

The circumstances of the breakup for Jack were overwhelming. His love for Jan had been shattered, his trust destroyed, and one of his deepest friendships betrayed. To make matters worse, the wound was never permitted to heal because Jack and Jan continued to see each other practically every day. Discreet avoidance was an impossibility due to their proximity. Jack owned a trailer park. He lived in a trailer at one end and she in a trailer at the other end. It was a small enough world that they saw and talked to each other every day.

In all their years of marriage, neither of them drank. The vices they both shared were perhaps too much coffee and too many cigarettes. In those years, caffeine and nicotine were more tolerated than frowned upon.

But now the pain raged like an inferno deep within Jack's soul. Finally the tears came. Late at night, and again with the start of yet another unwelcome, unwanted day, and again when the loneliness of night descended upon him.

He reached out for the bottle as a band-aid for his heart. It numbed the pain, it eased the burning, and it soothed the anguish. But the dawn of morning brought back the sting of reality far more painfully than the ache of the hangover.

As the months passed by, his depression worsened. Life seemed empty and meaningless. What was the purpose of pursuing the search for gold without someone to share the adventure? What was the purpose of pursuing life itself when it had become so barren and deserted?

Somewhere in the dark recesses of his troubled mind, a seed began to grow.

Jack made an appointment with his doctor.

"Hey doc, my nerves—they're real bad. Can't sleep, my stomach's botherin' me, and I get these headaches." He asked innocently, "You think you can give me somethin' to try and calm me down?"

It wasn't an unusual request from a patient. A routine physical examination showed no cause for any other medical concerns. Satisfied that it was a temporary problem, the doctor prescribed a reasonably potent tranquilizer that to the hulk of a man like Jack would guarantee relief from his complaints.

Satisfied, Jack got the prescription filled. Soon now, the time would come.

A week later, late in the evening, the usual bottle of Scotch had served to make him drunk enough and bold enough to end his life.

From the dresser drawer he extracted the prescription and downed six of the pills, more than triple the prescribed dosage. Then for good measure, he shook out another twenty of the thirty-pill prescription and downed those too. It was now a more than lethal dose. Committed to the last moments of his life, he lay down on his bed, head on his pillow, and quietly waited for unconsciousness and death.

But fate this time refused to cooperate. Unannounced and unexpected, less than thirty minutes after he'd overdosed, his son Richard from Calgary arrived by Greyhound bus, and made his way to his father's house. When there was no response to his knocking, he found his way inside to find Jack comatose on the bed. Alarmed when his efforts to wake him failed, he ran to a neighbor and when neither of them could rouse Jack, they called an ambulance and rushed him to hospital. For several hours, Jack's life hung in a balance.

He had teetered on the very edge of oblivion. When his life had been threatened before it had been the forces of man or nature against him. This time it had been his own doing. The next day when he was finally released from hospital he now had to live with both the remorse and the regret that he had failed to bring an end to his suffering. The pain was still there.

But one thing was apparent. The continued daily exposure to Jan was simply too painful. Jack made the decision to move to Revelstoke. Perhaps the separation and the distance between them would help heal the wound.

He made an attempt at bravado. He drank even more, partied, dated other women, and caroused long and hard. But there were many nights, drunk behind the wheel of his car, that he would look at a semitrailer approaching, a bridge abutment or the drop off into a ravine and consider how quickly he could put himself out of his misery.

Once, coming home in his usual inebriated state, he fell asleep at the wheel. The car went off the road, down a steep embankment and as it hit the bottom with considerable impact, Jack woke out of his stupor. Realizing that he'd left the road and that is where he ought to be, he gunned the accelerator and the car climbed back up the embankment, and sailed in midair over the shoulder and back onto the road. A motorist following cautiously behind later described the entire episode as that of something related to one of the more hair-raising of Hollywood's stunt driving scenes. But for Jack, fate had failed to play the card he most wanted.

Despite his attempts at bravado, his depression worsened. Seeing Jan hurt terribly. Being away from her hurt even more. Several months later, he returned to the trailer park. Jan still lived there and they resumed their casual encounters and their conversations. But the tears still came, the grief still remained unabated and the pain unstemmed. Once more he attempted to rid himself of this unending anguish.

This time he would not fail.

There would be no pills, no waiting, no medical intervention. This time it would be sudden, swift, and final.

He prepared the hangman's noose as carefully as he

could, tying the supporting end to an overhead beam. Next he handcuffed his wrists together and then centered the chair beneath the rope. Carefully he positioned the rope around his neck. Then, as the final act, he kicked the chair out from beneath him.

Jan was sitting in her living room talking to Roy, a nearby neighbor. It was a casual evening, with the usual coffee in front of her and a cigarette in her hand. Without warning, part way through her conversation, Jan stopped talking. Expectantly she turned her head as if sensing, testing the air. Then suddenly she spoke.

"Roy, something...something's wrong. I think it's Jack. I think he's in trouble. I need to know if he's alright." She quickly grabbed a sweater, and the two left and hurried through the night to Jack's trailer.

No response to their knocking. No response to their calls. Impulsively she rushed inside.

At the end of the rope, handcuffed, Jack was strangling. Unconscious and unable to get enough air to breath, he was moments from death. With only seconds left, they worked frantically to release the rope from around his windpipe and neck. As the first few breaths of air began to revive him, he looked up into her eyes. The tears were streaming down her face, his head was cradled in her lap and her hands were caressing his face. Between sobs, she told him she loved him and always would. That no matter what, he must never give up, he must never ever try to take his own life ever again.

For Jan's sake, he kept that promise.

18
Shadows of the Dream

And how many trips had there been to find the three peaks, the tent-shaped rock, and the creek that goes nowhere? From the moment he had read a copy of the letter that referred to those three signposts, they had become indelibly etched in his mind.

So profoundly rugged was the terrain he was pitting himself against, that it often seemed a fruitless and punitive endeavor to even hope of finding the gold. But surely, three peaks, a single tent-shaped rock, and a creek that goes nowhere should somehow, someday, align themselves in a position to disclose that elusive cache of gold.

Sitting at home in an armchair, reading tales of a legendary lost gold mine on a winter's evening is a pleasant pastime. Incurring the cost, accepting the danger, and devoting time, effort, and energies to explore such desolate and savage wilderness requires commitment. Once again, Jack reviewed the pitifully few clues upon which he was focusing his life.

Slumach. No doubt at all that he existed. The court records verify the Indian's trial and his hanging. But what else can be authenticated? Did he, in fact, actually discover the gold? Or did he simply trade the young girls he brought with him with the braves of the Hamathka tribe in exchange for nuggets? Unlike his own tribe who were hunters and fishermen, Slumach was a trapper. And trappers go where

121

animals go. High, remote, away from man, to a place where they are protected, a land they can claim as their own.

Rumors had floated around that Slumach would suddenly appear with gold nuggets that would launch him on one long drunken party, until sober and broke once again, he would quietly slip away without a trace. But this would not make headlines. This was hardly an event. It was unlikely that it would provoke even a simple entry in a diary or journal. So Jack was once again left to speculate on the cornerstone of evidence to support the belief in a lost gold mine.

As for the curse, Jack's mind reflected back on the times he'd been on the mountain. How many times had he gone in to that godforsaken land and how many times had he almost never returned? He was a man who, throughout his life, had taken on more than his share of risks and dangers both within and outside of jobs. He was an outdoorsman, familiar and aware of potential hazards. But what was that seemingly impenetrable force, that mysterious resistance that he had met so many times in the past? What was it that allowed him to overcome one obstacle and then suddenly be stopped by another? Yes, there were forces at work. But for a moment he pondered. Were they weakening? Would one day the curse simply die? Would it have lived out its appointed term and then release its strength and disappear? Or would it forever remain an obstacle? And if Jack continued to pursue—to get too close to what it guarded—would he simply be rendered another victim in the roll call of all those who had died before him?

The hair on his arms tensed and a small shiver washed over him. He'd pondered these thoughts so many times before. And the answers were always the same.

He was fighting more than the mountain. And some ...thing, was fighting back. To escape the uneasy thoughts he turned his attention to the next piece of evidence.

The most conclusive indication of the gold mine was the letter written by a John Jackson to a one-time sponsor who had grubstaked him earlier. Could the letter simply be a hoax? What was the real relationship between the two men? If it was sincere, then perhaps the letter was valid. Jackson had been an experienced and methodical prospector. He'd had maps and provisions and had remained in the mountain area north of Pitt Lake for several months. Upon his return, he had kept a watchful guard over a heavy pack before leaving New Westminster. Reportedly he had made a deposit of 10,000 dollars at the Bank of British North America in San Francisco shortly after arriving in the city. Then mysteriously he began to fall ill, a slow degenerating illness that ultimately warned him of his impending death. He knew he would never again journey back into the mountains to claim a fortune. But in a gesture of friendship, he composed and sent a letter giving the location of the gold by indicating the presence of a tent-shaped rock with a mark cut out of it, facing a creek that boils and bubbles out of the mountain and then some distance later, simply disappears. But even Jackson warns in the letter that "it is so well guarded by surrounding ridges and mountains that it should not be found for many years." And he warns his benefactor that even though he has described the location, "it may take a year or more to find it." The letter had been written on May 28, 1924 and reprinted here.

I had been out over two months and found myself running short of grub.

I had lived mostly on fresh meat for one can't carry much of a pack in those hills.

I found a few very promising ledges and colors in the little creeks but nothing I cared to stay with.

I had almost made up my mind to light out the next day. I climbed up to the top of a sharp ridge and looked down into the canyon or valley about one mile and a half long, and what struck me as singular, it appeared to have no outlet for the little creek that flowed at the bottom.

After some difficulty I found my way down to the creek.

The water was almost white, the formation for the most part had been slate and granite, but there I found a kind of schist and slate formation.

Now comes the interesting part.

I had only a small prospecting pan but I found colors at the site right on the surface, and such colors they were.

I knew then that I had struck it right at last.

In going up stream I came to a place where the bedrock was yellow with gold.

Some of the nuggets was as big as walnuts and there were many chunks carrying quartz. After sizing it up, I saw there was millions stowed around in the little cracks.

On account of the weight I buried part of the gold at the foot of a large tent shaped rock facing the creek.

You can't miss it.

There is a mark cut out in it.

Taking with me what I supposed to be ten thousand dollars (in gold) but afterwards it proved to be a little over eight thousand dollars.

After three days hard traveling, it would not have been over two days good going, but the way was rough and I was not feeling well, I arrived at the lake and while resting there was taken sick and have never since been able to return, and now I fear I never shall.

I am alone in the world, no relatives, no one to look after me for anything.

Of course I have never spoken of this find during all this time for fear of it being discovered.

It has caused me many anxious hours but the place is so well guarded by surrounding ridges and mountains that it should not be found for many years, unless someone knew of it being there. O, how I wish I could go with you to show you this wonderful place, for I cannot give you any exact directions, and it may take a year or more to find. Don't give up but keep at it and you will be repaid beyond your wildest dreams.

I believe any further directions would only tend to confuse it, so I will only suggest further that you go alone or at least only take one or two trusty Indians to pack food and no one need know but that you are going on a hunting trip until you find the place and get everything for yourself.

When you find it and I am sure you will, should you care to see me, advertise in the Frisco Examr., and if I am living I will either come to see you, or let you know where to find me, but once more I say to you, don't fail to look up this great property and don't give up until you find it.

Now goodbye and may success attend you.

These words were written over sixty-seven years ago. And in sixty-seven years, nature destroys and rebuilds, reshapes, and redefines. Snow, ice, wind, slides, avalanches, fire, and lightening. And the erosion of time itself. Had the creek disappeared? Had a slide changed its direction? And what of the tent-shaped rock? One unusually shaped rock in a mountain of rock? Was it not, too, the proverbial needle in a haystack? For most of the year the mountain was shrouded in ice and snow, too deep and too dangerous to penetrate. Only with the warm winds and the heat of the sun, did the snow finally melt away. But then it would be summer, and the months to explore the terrain before winter would be all too brief and few. One rock. One creek. In a world of mountain and snow.

Then there was the matter of the jar containing eleven ounces of gold. Volcanic Brown an experienced old prospector with a game leg would head into the headwaters of Pitt River and return in September or October, with gold nuggets. Where had he gotten them from? Then one autumn in 1930, he failed to appear. As the weeks passed and concern increased, a search party was finally mounted. It took twenty-seven grueling days in the face of subzero temperatures and full scale blizzards over glaciers and snowdrifts before they found his camp.

There was no trace of Volcanic Brown. But in the jar were the nuggets. Where had he stashed the rest of the gold that he had planned on bringing out? And where was it coming from?

Unlike Jackson, the legacy left by Brown was mute. No hint, no trace, no maps or letters were ever found. Only the eleven ounces of gold remained to tease, tantalize, and to entice one even deeper into the web of mystery.

Yet it had to be there. All the years of searching can't have been in vain. Slumach, Jackson's letter, Volcanic Brown. Unknowingly, they had shared a bond. How many others had there been who had also shared briefly that same bond, and had never lived to prove it?

19
Backseats and Bedsprings

In all his years of marriage Jack had been faithful to his wife. He'd never chased women. He'd never cheated. But he had the ability to attract more than his share of the ladies. Some time after the road to recovery following the breakup of his marriage, that had taken him over a year, Jack decided that maybe a lady or two, or three, or four, might put a little spice in his life and fill the empty void that haunted both his days and his nights. After all, he'd done the same thing after the breakup of his first marriage. At that time, he'd cultivated seven of them.

He'd spent one night of the week at each of the ladies houses, as he had explained to them, "as I'm only in town one night of the week." He had to remember to keep their names straight and his stories correct but otherwise it was a rather convenient if strenuous lifestyle. With his personal effects deposited at each of their homes, he'd been able to live a rather risque but carefree, as well as, rent-free existence.

So, once again, Jack began to cultivate his "trapline." Young, older, single, divorced, or married. Married women after all were a safer bet in that they were less likely to move in with him. According to Jack, when they live under the same roof, they get possessive. And they also get a tad ticked off to find out they're sharing his bed with a couple of other ladies at the same time they're in it! And besides, when his attention and his performances were required by five or six women, the relationships were less likely to get serious than if there was only one woman. Exhausting work, mind you, but it did have its benefits.

Jack cultivated a way with women that made him highly appealing. Out of bed, he treated women with care and attention. He loves to dance and is a very good dancer. He wines and dines them, takes them on shopping trips, to the race track or to the fights, or to theaters and concerts. Whatever the activity, he keeps them well entertained. His language that could easily curdle milk, becomes refined and gentile. His mannerisms, are both charming and flattering. Women are treated with respect and affection. And in bed, they're exposed to a very skilled lover who knows how and what to do to deliver them to undiscovered pinnacles of pleasure and satisfaction.

But he's a rogue.

He's also a little hard on the furniture. Namely beds. But then beds weren't particularly designed to support the antics of five women and a 230 pound man, frolicking the night away. The manufacturers of Simmons posturepedic mattresses probably had sleep in mind for their product. But to Jack, given the opportunity for a little touch and tickle time, sleep is simply out of the question. Unless of course, the evening revolves around a little skinny dipping in the backyard pool. Then the bed gets a rest and the pool-side lounge cushions take the beating. That at least helps save the bed, the sofa, the living room rug, and the kitchen table. All of which are well-anointed locations for dipping into the jam jar of erotic bliss. As for his bed, according to the manufacturers surveys, it should last an average of twenty years. Jack's bed uses up its warranty in about its first twenty minutes.

Sometimes the action gets mobile. As in the back of a chauffeured limousine driving down Georgia Street with a case of the finest bubbly, and five women who, except for the one way windows, might have been observed to be having an allergic reaction to their clothes.

Something about this gentle giant with his gravel voice and mischievous eyes, inspired more than one married woman to wander astray. One such lady simply walked out of her marriage and into Jack's life until he gently persuaded her to accept the error of her ways. It took several weeks of connubial coaxing mind you, but in the end she reluctantly returned to her family. Another married woman handled Jack a little more discreetly. Each morning, Monday to Friday, she would stop by Jack's house for coffee on her way to work. She performed her "service call" faithfully, for months on end, until for work related reasons, Jack left town. Yet for all his flirting and philandering, he is careful not to put himself or anyone else at risk. But that doesn't necessarily apply to making a date.

One day recovering from yet another all night party, Jack was almost asleep in the back of the limousine as it sped along the Upper Levels freeway from dropping off his ladies at the ferry terminal for their journey back to Vancouver Island. A casual glance to his right perked him awake. A very attractive lady flashed him a lovely vivacious smile as she maneuvered her pickup truck alongside the limousine. And with those devilish eyes of his, he responded back. For fifteen minutes, the limousine and the pickup truck played cat and mouse at 120 kilometers an hour in and out of very heavy ferry traffic. Then a business card appeared in the driver's window of the pickup. Impossible to get close enough to read it, Jack signaled her to come alongside. With her hand and his outstretched and with both vehicles only inches from each other the business card with the all important phone number passed from her hand to his. Two days later, he called her and made a date for dinner.

One would perhaps assume a quiet little restaurant with soft music and a candlelit table. Cocktails first and then dinner. Well almost. Soft music and candles yes. Cocktails and a catered dinner. Yes. And all of it served up in the back of the limo.

But while Jack's private life involved him in the rather rarified atmosphere of group dates and whatever else they led to, his business life had shifted direction.

The lost gold mine had once again become his obsession. Once again, he would begin his quest to find those elusive three peaks, the single tent-shaped rock, and the creek that goes nowhere.

20

Bears: Comics and Killers

Oddly enough, it began with a mouse.

Mark, Kelly, Jim Everett the dowser, and Jack, in the bush for a week to do some preliminary work, had set up camp. It included an ample supply of dry goods along with fresh meat, cases of canned salmon, cereals, breads, honey, peanut butter, and beverages. But camping did have it's hardships, petty as they might be.

Over the course of several meals, the mouse acquired a name, if somewhat by default. "Sam" became the abbreviation of son of a bitching m—— f—— along with every other colorful expletive that was hurled at the creature when yet another bag of pancake mix was found drilled by tiny but persistent teeth.

Sam of course was not only inviting himself to dinner but to breakfast and lunch as well, which became increasingly apparent with each meal. The telltale holes and his peppercorn-sized calling cards were evidence enough. Sam was becoming more than a pest. He was a tormentor, a plague in a one-ounce overcoat.

Four men. Four guns. Four days. The battle raged. The teeter-totter fight for Sam's survival grew ominous. The sound and fury of yet another shotgun blast sent Sam scurrying from the flour into the cake mix batter in search of a sanctuary. And to help him overcome his headache of course, he'd take a little sustenance on the side.

Clearly, Sam had found his very own gold mine in this apparently never ending gravy train. But it was also seriously endangering his wee neck.

Maybe there was a better way, he thought to himself—and a more vicarious way—to get to the goodies.

The day began early, around 5:00 A.M., with a breakfast of eggs, hotcakes, ham, and toast. The work to be done by the four men was hard and the terrain difficult, if not dangerous. By nightfall, they were hungry and tired. Finally, back at camp, they cooked and then wolfed down their dinner. Tired and mellow, sleep beckoned them to their tent.

The cold night air encouraged Mark, Kelly, and Jimmy to pull their sleeping bags over their heads. The dark, the quiet, and the exhaustion from the day's physical exertion was the corridor to oblivion. For Jack, nearest the door of the tent, it was also. With one exception.

For Jack, covers over his head were claustrophobic. Instead, he turned on his side to face toward the tent's outside wall and soon drifted off into a deep, sound sleep.

Was it an unfamiliar noise? An unexpected movement? Or was it an inner sixth sense that roused him from such a dead sleep?

From lying on his side facing the tent he turned slowly over to find a great black bear standing over him, barely inches from his face. Presumably the bear had entered the tent in search of food, and found instead four sleeping bags with only human occupants. As Jack's hands slipped slowly outside the sleeping bag to the .45 handgun and the 30-06 rifle lying beside him, the bear lumbered to the back of the tent and with one swipe of his paw, shredded the tent and disappeared into the night.

Jack shouted to the others. Quickly dressing, they began searching the area surrounding their camp.

The bear had vanished. There had been no sightings, no

evidence of bears in the vicinity. Yet their night, their tent, and their lives had been invaded without warning by a bear.

Unknown to them, the bear would be the precursor of the day yet to come.

* * *

With the approach of dawn the men roused themselves and began their usual breakfast routine. Midday the helicopter dropped off supplies to replenish their larder. The groceries were stored away in coolers and containers to see them through the rest of the week. For four hungry men on a mountain it meant an ample supply of food.

It was late afternoon when the first of them, Mark was to return to camp. Shortly thereafter, the three remaining men heard a shotgun blast and thoroughly alarmed, rushed back to camp. A large black bear lay dead beside what little remained of the cooler.

The camp itself was destroyed. Tents were ripped to shreds, clothes were strewn about and trampled, equipment chewed and broken, and food either eaten or contaminated. Wrappers from packages of T-bone steaks and pork chops trailed off into the bushes. Each tin in a case of canned salmon had been bitten or clawed open. Commercial-sized buckets of peanut butter and honey had been eaten and licked clean.

Almost the entire campground was white from the combination of bags of flour, sugar, cake, and pancake batter that had been torn open. And what hadn't been eaten lay wasted in the dirt.

The cooler, the size of a chest freezer, had had its lid ripped open and mangled, with its entire contents gone. For some inexplicable reason, only one item of the dozens destroyed remained intact. It was a plastic container of honey in the very shape of a bear! For a bear to preserve his own image would give him an intelligence he does not possess and perhaps even have us question our own. But the fact remained, it and it alone, survived intact. However, at the moment it was immaterial. What they surveyed in shock and disgust was quite literally a garbage dump.

As if to dishearten the men even more, a cold damp rain began to fall as the evening approached. It would be a night without food or shelter and little else to wear other than the clothes on their backs.

Concerned about their safety as night approached, they spread out and searched the area. From the tracks that were found, not one but four bears had destroyed their camp. The bruins had delivered not inconsiderable inconvenience, discomfort, danger, and expense. It would be two, long, cold and hungry days before the helicopter returned to replenish their supplies.

As for Sam, he was no longer wanted as the centerfold for the cross hairs of a shotgun. Now he had a feast of a lifetime to dine on to his little heart's content. He'd made it to mouse heaven!

* * *

This would not be the only encounter Jack was to have with bears. The next encounter could have ended with tragic results.

Jack and a business partner and friend, Dave Scrivens arranged to be dropped by plane into the site and later flown out by helicopter. It was a day meant for exploration. Equipped with backpacks, both men carried food, water, first aid kits, and their hiking equipment. Scrivens was an ex-RCMP officer trained in the use of firearms. Jack also had used weapons for hunting and self-defense all his life. It is ironic that on this particular trip, of all the times Jack had been into the wilderness, both men were without guns.

It was particularly ironic, too, that on this particular trip they came face to face with a grizzly.

Midmorning on a particularly cold and wet day, they had hiked out through a marsh to a clearing. Ahead of them some fifty yards, the grizzly lifted his head in their direction, alerted by their scent. The small beady eyes spotted the men and fixed them in a stare as it began to slowly move in their direction. The two men had spotted the bear at precisely the same moment and had stopped in their tracks. Jack slowly began to slip his back pack off and dropped it to the ground. Scrivens followed suit. Both of them were very aware there could be a confrontation and that they, without weapons, were defenseless. Very slowly they backed away, movements designed to lessen the appearance of a threat. Once back in the marsh, they bolted, hoping the bear would not give chase. When they had covered a considerable distance, they stopped briefly to catch their breath. When they looked back, they were even more alarmed. The bear was still behind them. By their scent it was tracking them down.

There was no easy escape. There were no trees that offered a suitable sanctuary. No shelter of any kind that offered protection. Once again they began to move, slipping through the underbrush toward a camp a remote distance away. For nearly an hour, as they fled, the bear followed. Even more menacing was the fact that their back packs had remained untouched by the grizzly.

Clearly it had had little interest in the food they contained. Jack and Dave had inadvertently wandered into what the bear considered to be his territory.

Finally, satisfied that the men were retreating out of his neck of the woods, the grizzly called off the hunt. Not sufficiently threatened to attack the men, it had nevertheless posed a deadly situation. Bone weary, they reached camp at twilight for much needed food and rest. The next day a helicopter dropped them temporarily back at the scene of their first sighting to retrieve their backpacks.

Strangely, they had remained untouched.

For all the trips into the mountain with his nephew, friends, and partners, their were many trips when Jack went in alone. A man used to the rugged wilderness, he, like the Indians, often wore moccasins rather than boots. Moccasins register the uncertain terrain better than boots and give a closer sense of what is underfoot. Along with his provisions and survival gear, he would usually carry a hunting knife, a handgun, and a shotgun or a rifle. Despite being armed and experienced, the strange uneasiness of those who had mysteriously disappeared or who had died shortly after returning from this mountain lurked in the back of Jack's mind. Fate had dealt too many mysterious happenings for Jack to entirely dismiss the haunting of the curse.

On this particular trip into the mountain by himself, he was watchful, alert, and cautious. One common element appears to run through the stories of people attacked by bears. The element of surprise. How a 1,200-pound animal can suddenly appear out of nowhere without warning seems impossible.

Yet case after case of maulings and death suffered at the hands of a bear that have been witnessed say that attacks are so sudden the victim, though often armed, hasn't the time to even fire his weapon.

Twigs snap. Leaves rustle. Branches groan. Creeks slither over gravel beds with wet whisperings. Sun and clouds hide behind trees and cast shadows of themselves like invisible enemies. Startled birds take sudden flight. And the rain and mist can shroud the world in a surrealistic tomb.

Across Jack's bull neck and shoulders, the hair began to rise like an antenna sensing a vague, distant danger. The sheer brute strength in his arms and legs suddenly sharpened for no apparent reason. He stopped. He listened. He scanned the underbrush around him. Silence. A deathly silence. Eerie. Nothing.

For several seconds, his senses monitored his surroundings, taking in the silence that now seemed so uncanny. Then again he began to move slowly, carefully through the dense underbrush toward the small clearing ahead.

The fallen fir tree was mammoth. Long dead, the moss grew like rich green fur, thick and luxurious over the bark. Treacherously slippery underneath the moss, the ground on either side of such logs is often booby trapped with rabbit holes of limbs and boughs of underbrush. Taking it like a fence to be climbed, Jack, from firm ground beneath him, heaved himself onto the top of the log. Then turning about face, he readied himself and jumped down backwards to the other side of the log. He turned to face the clearing.

She was standing less than ten feet away, the silvery gray fur of the telltale hump identifying her instantly as a grizzly. Dark beady eyes focused on Jack and a low huffing sound emanated deep within her massive chest. Suddenly the world was shredded by a thunderous growl as her mouth opened to expose the deadly white fangs. In the same instant, she suddenly moved two steps forward and then reared up on her hind legs, the massive front paws with their flesh wrenching claws raised and ready to tear. There was no time. In a second, no more than two, she would be on top of him.

His movements were precise, executed within the remaining split second. His right hand went to his side, slipped off the safety, found the trigger, and fired the sawed off shotgun directly from his hip holster. Her head, high and slightly turned ready to attack, was his target. With the blood curdling explosion of the shotgun, it found its mark.

She dropped and died instantly less than three feet from where he stood.

Twigs snap, leaves rustle, branches groan. In a story world of wilderness, these are the sounds that should be. But perhaps for a moment in time this world was suspended. Perhaps this was another story. A story about a man, and a curse.

21
Accident or Fate?

The beat of the rotary blades sliced open the sky and shredded the quiet of the late afternoon. It had been still and calm before the invading helicopter. The sun's fingers were reaching deep into the craggy crevices for the last of the winter's ice. The snow had gone, the blizzards past, the rain and fog, temporarily in abeyance.

The throbbing of the rotor blades seemed as though they were inside his head.

Jack sighed deeply, lowered his head to his hands and pressed his finger tips to his temples. For a moment it helped to ease the tension. Then he once again lifted his head and went back to scanning the rocks, trees, and bushes on each ridge they passed.

It was a maze of crevices, valleys, ridges, and cliffs. From every angle the mountain took on a new perspective, as if it wore a different mask from each angle. The helicopter hovered, then drifted, moving along invisible corridors in the sky, a dragonfly seeking it's prey.

So many attempts. So many failures. It was late in the day and the sun's lengthening shadows played cat and mouse games that made observation all the more difficult.

They had been over the area countless times before. It seemed they had been over the entire mountain hundreds of times before. How could it look so different? How could it be so unfamiliar? They had seen the mountain crested with eight, ten, fifteen feet of snow drifted against the cliff facings. And they had seen it barren, as it was now.

For a brief moment, Jack's mind wandered back to a particular part of the mountain. One that had come close to costing him his life.

He had been with Jimmy and Mark. They were working their way down the mountain when Jack decided to go off by himself and cover an unexplored area. It was never wise to travel into that kind of wilderness by oneself, but then often he had no choice. Opportunities were rare. The season and the weather created far too few windows to pass up a chance.

On this particular trip, he'd undergone surgery to have his gallbladder removed the week before. Where he really should have been was at home convalescing. Instead he was clamoring over a mountain, alone in a hostile and unpredictable terrain.

He was wearing boots, not the usual moccasins he normally wore. And his mind and his movements were focused on motions that would not aggravate the pain of his surgery.

Accidents wait to happen. They seize the opportunity of a moment's brief inattention to their surroundings and simply bide their time.

Suddenly, the foothold of rock beneath his feet gave way and he was rolling, out of control down the side of the mountain with nothing to stop him. Frantically he grabbed at anything to stop his fall. Nothing held. Then in terror he plunged over the edge of a cliff.

By a miracle, he landed on a narrow ledge that would only have broken but not stopped his fall, had it not been for one solitary tree that prevented him from continuing over the side.

Shaken and in pain, minutes passed before he cleared his head, then gradually observed his position.

He'd fallen approximately forty feet to a ledge that,

while eight or nine feet in length, was less than two-feet wide. Below the ledge was a clear 1,000-foot drop, and certain death.

There was no way back up. There was no way down. And there was nowhere else to go.

The pain pills helped. He had made sure that he'd at least taken enough of them along.

He shot the guns off to let Jimmy and Mark know he was in trouble.

Air, Sea and Rescue would fly surveillance of the mountain. A search party would be manned and dropped off by helicopter to search the mountain. And if the weather deteriorated and cloud moved in, which was highly likely, given the location, the season, and the climate, it could be days before he was located.

It was a decidedly dismal prospect. Without food, water, or shelter he would quickly deteriorate. Once his pills were depleted he would be in intense pain both from the surgery and from the fall itself. And any careless movement to keep himself warm or to ease his body from discomfort and pain, or sleep if mercifully he could, would risk a fall over the edge to oblivion. He would have to use his belt somehow to secure himself to the tree. And he would have many long hours to reflect on the gold, the mountain, and the curse.

The minutes seemed hours. Each time he checked his watch, the hands seemed frozen in the same place they had been before. He was getting hungry. He was getting restless. And he was getting worried.

Very distantly what seemed like a giant moth, beat its wings. It was a low muffled sound almost like thunder from somewhere very far away. The direction of the sound was confusing. It seemed all around him, but distantly remote. Very gradually the cadence changed to a rhythm above a drone. Suddenly he knew! Tension changed to excitement and he climbed to his feet urgently examining the skies. The beating of the rotor blades above the engine of the helicopter now became distinct as it grew closer. At first, no more than a fly speck in the sky, it began to take form. Closer and closer it came till it was hovering directly overhead. He could see the pilot working the controls and he watched excitedly as the rescue line was lowered carefully and precisely down to the ledge where Jack was waiting.

Within minutes he was inside the helicopter. The pilot and Jack shouting greetings which were left unheard over the noise of the rotor and the engines. Then the machine curtsied her good-bye and fled the mountain.

Jimmy and Mark had taken the rope and the pack with the radio with them. They, too, had had a bit of trouble and had dropped the pack with the radio in it. Although the radio broke, they were able to fix it. After four hours, they realized something was wrong and reported Jack missing.

As it turned out, Air, Sea and Rescue was already involved in another search, so they called Pemberton Helicopter instead. Jack had been on the ledge eight and a half hours and once saved, the rescue operation cost him 1,500 dollars.

Again the curse had threatened to make him a victim, but failed. Why, when so many had died, was Jack once again spared?

Or was it simply that his time had not yet come?

22
Victory!

The thudding of the helicopter's engine seemed to penetrate inside Jack's head like the incessant pain of a migraine headache. For some peculiar reason this trip in, he felt a sense of futility, as though he was already living the disappointment and frustration of all the previous trips. Why would this trip be any different? How many more trips would there be before he would be forced to accept failure? Forced to recognize that this lifelong quest was a mere dream, a search for a fortune in gold that would remain hidden perhaps for all time. There had been times before, countless times like this that he would have been filled with hope, with excitement, tingling with anticipation. Terrain he had dangerously and painstakingly covered on foot, he could see now in a single glance from the sky. From the helicopter, he had a perspective he could never achieve on the ground. And always, from the air, he had hoped for that one angle that would give him the glimpse of the three peaks. If only he could spot the three peaks, then surely he could find the tent-shaped rock and the creek that went nowhere. If he found those landmarks, then he knew he would find the gold. But even now, the mountain remained, as always, a treacherous maze of crevices and cliffs, rugged and hostile as always.

"Jack! Jack?"

Lost in memory, it took him a few brief moments to

respond. He was being called by the pilot of the helicopter, Craig Houston, who seemed preoccupied with something beyond Jack's line of sight. He had to pull his thoughts back from the mountain, the fall, the ledge, and the long fearful hours he'd spent alone waiting, hoping to be rescued.

More and more his mind seemed to focus on the memories of the mountain. The years and years of dangerous treks into this godforsaken terrain. The endless sacrifices. The physical risks. The staggering financial costs. For what? A lifelong pursuit of a dream that had destroyed the lives of so many others. A fortune in gold, silently guarded by a legendary curse who, like a teasing, tantalizing seductress lured men to their deaths. There had been so many that had perished. And so many times that he himself had almost met the same fate.

The mountain had seen him as a youth, vigorous, naive, strong. It had witnessed his maturity and with it, the dedication, the desire, the ambition. Now his bones had begun to feel the cold and his body had grown weary. And now even his spirit acknowledged the whisperings of the curse. Over the many long years, there had been those who shared if but briefly, the flame of his ambition, his dreams. But like the flame, many had burned briefly, and turned to ashes. For the most part, it had been a long and solitary search. Surely, God, the end must be near.

"Jack!" This time the voice was very loud, demanding an immediate response.

"Yeah, whatdaya got?" he shouted back over the whine of the chopper, as he turned awkwardly in the seat to try and bring the area Craig was looking at, into line.

"Just a minute, lemme get the angle right..." Craig shouted in reply. His hands and feet fine tuned the controls and the helicopter rose and circled in response.

"There! Take a look...your side."

Jack maneuvered back to his original position and

144

peered intently at what was lining up in front of him. Suddenly his entire body tensed. His eyes fixed trancelike at what he was seeing. Then uncontrollably he started to speak, which instantly crescendoed in pitch with joy.

"Well Jesus Christ! I'll be. There it is! Can you believe it? THERE IT IS!" Jack was shouting at the top of his lungs, jubilantly, triumphantly, his eyes greedily locked in place staring out and below.

In the distance, three peaks had aligned themselves in a row, not randomly, not casually, but precisely. Directly in front of them almost delicately positioned stood a tent-shaped rock, unmistakable in a conical pose. Beyond the rock, the white frothing gurgle of the creek bubbled out of the side of the rock face, raced down the side and then simply disappeared.

23
The Magic Man

The small gold nugget encased in its tiny container, called a witness pendulum, drifted in an arc over the map of Bute Inlet and the mountain range it bordered. His dark eyes were intense, his concentration focused. From his hand which suspended the pendulum, he waited for the first shiver of vibration. Seldom had he failed when he had been put to the test. And somehow he knew, deep down, he would not fail this time....

There! He felt it. There again! He was sure. Then he turned to the man who had approached him. Only a week ago Jack Mould had said that at last, after a lifelong search, he had finally located what he believed was Slumach's legendary lost gold mine.

But he had been given no indication on the map of the location. It had simply been placed before him, a meaningless maze of mountainous terrain, convoluted peaks and valleys with no beginning, no end. As always it was a test of his powers, a challenge to his abilities.

Carefully he pinpointed it on the map then turned to Jack, "Gold...three veins...huge ones...on the ridge here, and here, and one here on the Southgate Peak."

Miles from the location and with nothing but a nugget of gold and a map of the area, Jim Everett had pinpointed the precise location of the veins of the legendary lost gold mine!

146

* * *

Hoax, witchcraft, or crystal ball? To most people, the art of dowsing is, according to Jim, "just as mysterious and intriguing."

As a boy growing up in northern Ontario with his father and his uncles who were dowsers, he gave dowsing a token and unsuccessful try, then quickly lost interest. For the next thirty-odd years it continued to be of little importance to him. Then, when he moved to Vancouver Island, ten years ago, thoughts of dowsing began to drift back into his mind. He began to read. He began to study. He began to dowse. Ten years later, he has more than adequate proof of his "divine gift."

According to Jim, this gift, because of its mystique, should belong in the Middle Ages, but in fact it dates back as far as 8,000 years. As an ancient art, it has been practiced through the centuries. At times, it was covertly used when it became associated with the devil's work. Then it would redeem itself on the side of piousness and once again gain acceptance. Despite our world of technology it is still very widely used today.

"In early times dowsers were considered blessed with some kind of magical power," says Jim, "and it was in their interests to preserve that revered status. Today, dowsers are less secretive, though just as mystifying, I'm sure, to most people. But now there's a greater acceptance of our powers. Of course there are still nonbelievers and skeptics, but if someone wants water, bad, and I find it for them, then the proof is in the pudding."

That Jim Everett should have been able to detect the presence of gold from a map, for a dowser is not unusual.

"Most commonly, dowsers or diviners locate sources of underground water. One Vancouver Island man dowsed

147

and then personally dug by hand, sixty-one wells. Sixty of them produced water."

In attempting to better understand the mystique in dowsing, I had an in depth discussion with Jim on the subject.

I confronted Jim about a situation that had occurred in the 1800s in Waterford, England. It seems a factory in growing need of more water for its operation had a well dug to the depth of sixty-two feet believing they'd find water. When that well failed to produce, they consulted a professional company who, after taking soundings and geological surveys indicated the spot they felt would prove successful.

They bored down a distance of 292 feet without success. The next year, the company taking the most professional advice they could find, continued to bore to 612 feet through extremely difficult strata, to no avail. Three hundred and thirty-three feet deeper, with a well depth of over 1,000 feet, they still hadn't found water.

Desperate to resolve their problem they consulted the English dowser John Mullins who agreed to try.

Once on the factory site, knowing nothing of the effort and expense the company had already invested, he silently walked the site holding his divining rod. Only yards from the abortive bore hole, his divining rod twisted and broke.

"Water will be found here at the depth of around ninety feet," he informed the astonished owners.

Then he further indicated three other locations nearby as well that would produce water. The well was dug and an abundance of water was found just under the ninety foot level.

"Is dowsing the physical manifestation of extrasensory perception?" I asked.

Jim was quick to point out, "Dowsing for water is only one aspect of this uncanny approach to searching and discovering. It extends to predicting the weather, guiding a ship, finding minerals, oil, lost treasure, graves, bones, missing people, murders, illnesses, diseases, and even determining the sex of an unborn child.

"Many dowsers are limited by their abilities to only one or two areas. While finding the location of underground water is vital if there is no other source, locating significant deposits of ores such as gold, silver, and other precious minerals often pinpoints remarkable wealth that would otherwise remain undiscovered."

For centuries, the dowser with his divining rod was in wide practice throughout Europe locating precious minerals as well as water.

Through those same centuries, the Spaniards had used divining rods to locate gold, and were known to be dowsers. It was something that the North American Indians knew nothing about. Any wonder then, that the Spaniards when exploring the west coast of British Columbia and seeing the occasional gold nugget, would use their familiar method for tracking down deposits?

I reminded him of another case. An American company that was involved in industrial mining in the Middle East. Though they had selectively chosen eight sites in a wide expanse of land, they called in Robert Leftwich a dowser with an outstanding reputation to test their choices. From a plane flying over the vast distances, he studied the terrain below. Without a single clue to mark their proposed sights, he picked seven sights identically the same as the ones the company had already preselected! The eighth site, which he had not picked, later proved worthless.

Jim's response was predictable. A mere shrug of the shoulders. To a dowser, why should there be any doubt as to their abilities?

Though often skeptical, police investigators have had to reluctantly credit dowsers with locating a body when their own men had been unable to find it through their own searches.

William Wilks in his book, *Science of a Witches Brew* describes a particularly tragic incident. His niece, a well-known poet had been missing for some time. If she was dead, the whereabouts of her body had not yet been discovered. Wilks obtained a few of her hairs from a brush and took a fix on her location. It pointed to the general area of the University of British Columbia, which she often frequented. A few days later when he made the trip to the university campus in Vancouver from his home on Mayne Island, he was amazed to find his second bearing taking exactly the opposite direction. With trepidation, he called the police and learned that her body was in the morgue. The morgue was located at the direction of the bearing he had just been given.

Later, when he reexamined his original bearing it led up past the University to Howe Sound to a place called Furry Creek. It was from there that the police had recovered her murdered body.

One of the most fascinating cases Jim recounted to me is described in the book *Pendulum Power* by Greg Nielson and Joseph Polansky.

It seems that a professional dowser by the name of Verne Cameron contacted the U.S. Navy offering to identify the location of every submarine in the U.S. fleet. A few months later, he received a letter from Vice Admiral Curtis.

In it he wrote, "I am advised you believe you may be able to tell the location of all the submarines in the world's waters...and their nationalities by a technique called 'map dowsing.' It has been suggested you be given an opportunity to confirm your ability on the subject of submarine detection and location at a naval establishment close to you.

"Please be assured I should welcome a demonstration by you at a place of your choice on the west coast.

"If you will communicate with me about your itinerary

for the next month or so and your choice of a place where you can demonstrate this ability, I shall be pleased to arrange a test."

The meeting between Cameron and the Vice Admiral was arranged. Within minutes, to the astonished audience, Cameron pinpointed the exact location of each U.S. submarine in the entire fleet! Then he proceeded to pinpoint every Russian submarine in the world! Despite this incredible and shocking demonstration, Cameron did not hear from the navy again. Years later the South African government invited Cameron to visit their country in order to detect some natural resources. When he went to obtain a passport, his application was denied. Eventually, upon his own investigation, he learned that the navy had contacted the CIA and they had classified him as a risk to national security!

The medical profession has also been loathe to acknowledge the accuracy of a diagnosis made by a medically untrained and inexperienced individual, whose talent lies in such an unconventional and unscientific field as dowsing.

Jim dowsed an elderly man and found a blockage in his left leg between his knee and his thigh. Doctors confirmed it and treated him accordingly.

"It's not the kind of thing I really want to do though," Jim says. "I'm not a doctor, and I can't and won't do more than to pinpoint the problem. It's up to the doctors to fix it."

There are other things Jim won't do. And there are some things he can't do.

"I dowsed a sunken ship once—sank about 1874. I counted 270 people that went down with her. I know they're dead...long dead...but it still bothers me.

"Another time I dowsed a cave and we found the skeletons of thirty bodies...without their heads. Haida probably killed them. But I didn't feel good about that either.

"And I can't dowse lottery tickets. Just can't. I can dowse

a winning horse...for somebody else. But not for me. See, the gift has got to be used to do good, to benefit something or someone. If you use it to only make yourself rich or powerful, if you get greedy, then you'll lose it.

"Knew a dowser once. He was real good. Then he got greedy, real greedy. It was just disgusting to watch him. Then one day it was gone. He lost the gift. Just couldn't dowse anymore. It's not just me saying it. I belong to the American Society of Dowsers. It's kind of like our creed."

According to the bibles on dowsing, history has put before our eyes hundreds, thousands, of fully authenticated and documented cases of the consistent if unbelievable and repeated successes that dowsers experience.

A handbook on dowsing will tell you anyone can learn how to dowse. It's technique and it's practice. Another handbook suggests it's the fine tuning of the analytical brain, an acute awareness of one's surroundings, and highly developed levels of concentration. If, indeed, we were all capable of executing such precise and accurate observations, we no doubt would have readily resolved most of life's little inconveniences. Bank overdrafts, misplaced car keys, the whereabouts of our hyperactive five-year old. But it would appear that if we all have the potential to develop these abilities, they lie undeveloped and dormant in the majority of us mere mortals.

"It's practice, it's analytical thinking, it's concentration," Jim insists. "Probably everybody could do it, if they developed their capabilities. I'm good, much better than when I started, and each day I'm getting better. Most dowsers dowse for water. Considerably fewer dowse for minerals. And fewer still can dowse from a map. Most dowsers must walk every inch of the property. I can stand in one place and point. To dowse a well probably takes me ten minutes. Location, depth, and the number of gallons per minute. Costs them the price of a good dinner. To drill and put in casings is about twenty dollars a foot. So a well can run from 2,000 dollars to 10,000 dollars. Gets expensive if they don't find water. I'm ninety-eight to ninety-nine percent right."

A quiet competent man in his late fifties, with a gentle, good-natured manner, Jim Everett, is, in numerous trades a highly skilled tradesman.

He is a carpenter by trade, experienced in everything from house framing, cabinet construction, renovations, to wood carving. He has been a subcontractor building condominiums; a plant manager building cranes; a millwright welder in a plywood mill; a welder in a machine shop; a machinist in a machine shop; a production manager in a lighting fixture manufacturing plant; a tool and die maker for a refrigeration manufacturer; and a machinist for a tool and die manufacturing company. An impressive work history.

His passion, though, is dowsing.

His track record is even more impressive.

In his own handwritten records, scribbled in almost shorthand form, are the briefest mention of some quite astounding finds.

From his diary, we find these notations:

Princess Jade Mines and Store,
Highway 37, Cassiar Junction, Cassiar, B.C. V0C 1E0.
Location: Turnagain River Cassiar Region 1986.
Dowsed map. Found large grade A boulder plus large deposits. Also area where he was working. Confirmed spring/87.
Arrived June on location. Dowsed mountain. Marked deposits. Grade A jade. Still being confirmed.
Sold mine to Exon Mines which are still working area. $4,000.00

Ron
Employee of Jade mine. Cat operator. Private claim.
Cassiar area. French River.
Dowsed map. Placer gold—platinum.

153

Confirmed. Assay Office. Cassiar.
Later sold claim.

Mr. Frank Plutt, Prince Rupert.
Location: Turnagain River. Cassiar Region.
Dowsed claim for grade A jade.
Confirmed. Success. Sold to Exon Mines.

Mr. Paul Brasseau, Squamish, V0N 3O0.
Location: Rosewall Creek, Vancouver Island.
Dowsed map. Asbestos, copper, hard-rock gold.
Confirmed on site. Assay report.

Mr. R. Van Horne, Langley, B.C. V3A 4P6.
Location: Whipsaw Creek, Princeton area.
Dowsed map. Placer gold, platinum.
Small showing in fall. Resume in spring.

Cypress Bowl—Ron Supervisor. (Aviation Restoration
Club, Vancouver.)
Location: Twin Peaks area.
Dowsed map for crashed aircraft.
Confirmed. Club removed parts of aircraft.

Mr. Larry Delamore, Clearbrook, B.C.
Location: Quatsine Sound Lawn Point.
Located on map crashed aircraft.
Confirmed by Mr. Delamore.

Mr. Mike Lawrence, Errington, B.C.
Location: various creeks and areas.
Map dowsing then on location.

Mr. Jose' Morales, Buenvista de Cuellar, Guerreo, Mexico.
Location: ancient Maya ruins—Spanish mine.
Dowsed for gold and artifacts. Successfully found gold
and magnificent artifacts at exact location indicated on
map.

To peek briefly behind just two of these notations, we find
an amazing treasury of wealth, all uncovered by dowsing.

Jim was asked to dowse for jade. He first dowsed the map and then pinpointed the same location on the site. What was uncovered and dug out was one giant boulder weighing eleven tons of grade A jade! It sold for 225,000 dollars.

He was asked to dowse for jade again. He located what was to be later called the Great China Wall. That find was so good that the partners earned two to three million dollars apiece, the major shareholder four million dollars!

He says, "It's not only pinpointing the location of the mother lode to mining companies, but the enormous expense they are spared in the cost of test drilling. Even with all the most sophisticated surveys, analyses, and tests, the drilling still has to be done. It's expensive business. Millions can be spent in an exceedingly short time, all to no avail."

With this kind of talent to detect such wealth at his fingertips, why isn't he a wealthy man? Like most of us, he wishes he was.

"But the gift is indeed special, and very precious. I believe it comes from a supreme power. A force field, an energy field. Maybe even God. I haven't asked God, so I don't know. The others aren't even about to talk to me. No matter. The wealth I uncover doesn't matter. As word of my power spreads, my fees which are pretty modest now, will align themselves with the industry's standards for precious minerals and ores. X number of dollars per day plus expenses—then, a 10,000 dollar finder's fee and one percent royalty."

He lounges back in his armchair and savors the thought of so much money. A bigger house for his wife Eleanor, that long awaited holiday, financial help to a couple of needy grandchildren? Well, maybe.

The chair snaps to a salute as he suddenly can no longer sustain his fondest desire.

"If I really had the money, you know what I'd do?" His

eyes shimmered with excitement—with exuberation. "I'd be on the first plane that would take me to India...to the Middle East...to Africa.

"I'd find them water...darn, I'd find them water! And plenty of it. So all them people... all those women with their children and their babies... wouldn't get sick and die because there wasn't enough water to keep them healthy and there wasn't enough water to drink, to keep them from dyin'...."

24
On the Mark

Impatiently, Jack watched the weather and waited. Stubbornly, the skies remained overcast, shrouded in cloaks of gray as if they, too, had sided with the forces to prevent this man access to the mountain. The spring came and slipped into early summer. Still the mountain hid in icy crevices and snowy ledges. Then reluctantly, they melted away as the summer sun reached deep into the earth and encircled the mountain in her warmth.

They were ready to go.

The helicopter pilot, Jack, and Jim took off and flew over the mountain range to the tip of Bute Inlet. As the helicopter climbed and circled the Southgate peaks. Silently observing, Jack remained quiet.

Jim had been told nothing about the area, nothing about the three critically important landmarks. He would have to rely on that uncanny vibration of his dowsing rod to pinpoint the location of the veins.

Directly ahead of them, Jack saw the first of the three peaks come into view. The tension began to grow.

There was the second peak. And there was the third. His eyes shifted momentarily to Jim's face. Jim remained impassive yet his expression was creased with concentration. Then, coming into view, was the unmistakable profile of the tent-shaped rock. Soon they would be over the site, in moments beyond it. Once again he turned to Jim.

Silence.

Then suddenly the dowser spoke over the throbbing of the engine, "Over to the right, there, along that ridge...that's your vein. Stay to the right. It's there. Right there."

For a second he paused, then once again he spoke. He'd shifted his line of sight and was looking down at a ridge running at angles to the first. "That one, there's your second vein, and it's big...maybe twelve, fourteen feet wide."

One more time, he turned and pinpointed a ridge at a lower elevation than the first. "And there's the third."

The locations he had picked from the air were identical to the areas he'd dowsed on the map.

Elated at the news, it did not however, come as a surprise to Jack. As the helicopter rose further into the air and circled, once again the three peaks lined themselves up, the tent-shaped rock came into view, and cresting the peak on the other side was the creek that goes nowhere.

25
Shadows of the Past

Jim wore a troubled expression. He was staring at the same map that he had dowsed to find the gold veins. It was a week later and Jack had been making arrangements to fly Jim back into the site with the hope of being able to put down on the site itself.

Jim got up, went to a drawer and extracted a tiny pendulum made from a fishing lure that he placed over the map. It swung gently in an arc.

For many minutes caught up in total concentration, he was silent. His head was bent and his brown eyes focused on one small area of the map. Finally he lifted his head and spoke.

"Bones. Human bones. They're there. They're old. They're no longer a complete skeleton, but some parts are there. They've been there a long time."

"How many Jim, can you tell?" Jack asked, his curiosity piqued. Now that he had found the location of the mine, anything in the area was going to be of immense importance. Historically it could be a graveyard of artifacts. "Can you tell how old they are?"

"No...no I can't. But if we can find them, then we can find out how old they are."

"Can you find them for us, Jim, on the mountain?" As always the dowser's abilities struck Jack with awe.

With calm reassurance he spoke in his gently modulated voice. "I can find them for you."

With the same quiet confidence, three weeks later, Jim stood on a small pinnacle of rock and surveyed the terrain of the mountain. Calmly he pointed to the base of a cliff overhang. "Some of the bones will be there." It'll be a steep climb down but at least the area is accessible.

Again Jim pointed off in another direction.

"There, by those rocks." Once more he turned in yet another direction. "Over there, you'll find more."

It was a talent that not many dowsers had. Most would have to walk each inch of the terrain before they could detect what they were searching for. For Jim, he had only to stand in the given area and it became known to him.

It was both difficult and tiring work. It took several hours before they had climbed over the rough terrain to each location.

In each of the locations were bones. Old bones. Human bones.

Once again in remote, rugged wilderness, Jim Everett had found precisely what he had expected to find, by dowsing.

Of the bones they had recovered, one was later identified as the pelvis of a fourteen-year-old girl, likely a native Indian.

Another set of bones was identified as belonging to a smallish man, probably a white man rather than a native.

The last were leg bones, one with an obvious deformity.

All the bones had suffered the ravages of animals, weather, erosion, and time.

Jack submitted the bones for examination to the coroner's office. They, in turn, were handed over to Dr. James Ferris, professor of Forensic Pathology for further evaluation.

In a letter written October 23, 1989, Dr. Ferris replied

with his report to the coroner. In detailed medical terminology he described each of the bones recovered from the site.

His eighth paragraph reads: "All of these six bones show loss of bone density, extensive postmortem erosion and some calcium carbonate replacement. The general impression is that all of these bones are at least fifty years since death and may be up to 200 years since death. It was not possible on the basis of this examination to determine race, however, they would be consistent with native Indian. The indications are that this individual (referring to the last set of bones) had a very strong, powerfully developed upper body and may have had a pelvic and right leg bone abnormality, possibly as a result of old injury or congenital disease."

Were, in fact, these bones living proof of history itself?

Were the bones, presumably belonging to that of a smallish man, actually that of a Spaniard? If the Spaniards had mined gold in that area, treacherous as it was then and still is, some would have lost their lives. Some would have met their fate at the hands of destiny and simply gone missing, their fate never determined, their remains never found.

And the pelvic bone of a fourteen year old girl? How, why, would a mere child ever be in such a desolate, remote and distant location? She could not have possibly, or conceivably, become lost, disorientated, run away or fled for whatever reason and have found herself in such a location.

Perhaps we need to look back at both history and the legend.

History tells us that Slumach was hanged for the murder of the half-breed Louis Bee. But long before he was criminally documented for that crime, he was reputed to have taken Indian maidens—young girls who were barely adolescents with him to take care of both him and the tedious task of finding and recovering his gold nuggets. Each young woman he took in was never seen again. Is it odd then, that the remains of this child should be found in such a remote and desolate spot?

The leg bones bearing the misshapen abnormality are perhaps the most significantly strong link to the history of this cursed place.

One man, had many, many years ago, in the 1920s, attempted to find this elusive treasure of gold. He had journeyed in year after year, until the time he failed to reappear. That had been after he'd saved the life of likely his own murderer, a man intent on getting Brown's gold for himself. It cost Brown his toes, as they had become frostbitten and gangrenous. He cut them off to save his life. For the rest of his life he remained a cripple.

Were these the leg bones of the missing Volcanic Brown? Who else with such a crippling disability, would ever have a purpose or a reason to climb into such god forbidding country?

Perhaps then, the remains are indeed those of Volcanic Brown himself, who knew and who had found the legendary lost gold mine. A man who lost his own life in his search for gold—another mysterious victim who trespassed into the shadow of the curse.

26
Ending or Beginning?

She was being raped. Unrelentingly, slowly, but savagely. He and the others were penetrating her body, her soul, her spirit.

She had fought her whole life, to keep what was deep within her, to herself. So many had tried to take it from her and failed. With help, she had remained almost unseen, untouched, virginal. But unlike the others, this one man, again and again had tried to find her, searching, seeking and finally uncovered her—at the time when she was most defenseless.

She had cried a river of tears. They too ironically, had trailed her whereabouts and scented her location. Deep within her womb, she had desperately tried to protect her child. She had hidden it well, in winter, and in storms and always at night. But now, she lay before him, helpless and pleading.

She uttered one last cry to the heavens, to the sky. "Help me, please help me!"

She had had a protector. He had served her well through the years, standing invisibly on guard, sensing threats, diverting danger, at times, confronting the invader. Had he abandoned her now, or grown weak, perhaps even grown old and weary.

"Oh please, great spirit, protect me now in my hour of need!" She whispered her plea, her face turned upwards to the sky, searching and beseeching the heavens for deliverance from hell.

* * *

With undying persistence, Jack had plotted and planned what he hoped might well be the final assault. Everything would hinge on the results of this particular trip. All the years of frustration, despair, effort, and energy that had been expended, would now hopefully pay off. It had taken him hundreds of thousands of dollars and most of his life to bring him to the point where he was right now. Surely, this would finally prove successful. Surely, at long last, he would find the gold.

How many years had it taken him to locate the three peaks, the tent-shaped rock, and the creek that goes nowhere? How many more trips had it taken with Jimmy dowsing the area to pinpoint the veins? How many ore samples had they drilled for and how many geological surveys had had to be done?

There had been reporters, and curiosity seekers, the believers and the disbelievers, the promoters, the investors, and the con men and the scam artists. They had drilled, and finally staked their claims. Yet even now, as close as they were, they still were not finished. They would have to drill and trench till they had sufficient proof that enough gold existed for either an investor to finance a drilling operation, or drill to recover some of the gold for themselves.

Or, he could sell out to a mining company. This though, seemed the last option. He'd already explored that route. What he would likely be paid for his claims would be only a fraction of what they were worth. No, his nephew Kelly, and his brother Bill would keep the main ownership between themselves. Shareholders were limited in another company owning interest in the property, but they were very much in the minority.

So their work was cut out for them. Jack had known this and had planned accordingly.

First, in defining the areas he, Kelly, Mark, and Jimmy intended to work, he had had to first locate a campsite. It had to be near an adequate supply of fresh water, have reasonably suitable terrain and be large enough to accommodate their equipment. In order to meet those requirements, he then had had to fall enough trees to make a clearing for the helicopter they would use for transporting their supplies.

With the help of his cousin Roy, they had stowed two boatloads of groceries and provisions and sailed into Bute Inlet. Then, with time consuming effort, they had had to transfer the supplies to the beach, ready for the helicopter to move them to the site.

The helicopter itself made its first trip in, loaded fully with a cargo net as well, packed with supplies. Jack's mattress crested the heap. Sleeping on the ground in a sleeping bag, was not Jack's cup of tea. If he was going to have to wrestle with a mountain all day long, day after day, he was at least going to sleep at night in comfort. And, when the weather conditions were good, was when he had to be on the site. He remembered his last trip in and shuddered at what had nearly happened to him then. He hadn't been the only one to fall. A year ago in April, Kelly had nearly lost his life.

He and Kelly had taken in a movie camera to record the site of the claims. Snow still clung to crannies and crevices, leaving the rock face slippery and treacherous. Without warning, Kelly lost his footing. He plunged eighteen yards down the mountainside, before managing to stop his fall. He was only thirty feet from the edge of a 7,000-foot drop. Coming after so many previous incidents, it had been a terrifying experience. Once again the curse seemed more than real, delivering as it had throughout the years the warning to stay away from the gold.

Would there be another warning? Or would simply the next fall be fatal?

As the helicopter strained to takeoff, it made a heart stopping lurch forward, running across the ground at a dizzying angle, rapidly reducing the distance it had for take-off before the end of the beach. Then, as it began to finally climb, the men sighed with relief. In the backs of their mind, each man's thoughts lingered briefly again on the curse. A helicopter accident would very tidily snuff out all their lives. Each day they spent on the mountain seemed to bring the risk that much closer. And now they were going for several weeks. Just how much more could they tempt their fate?

It had taken an entire day in early June to establish camp at the site near the 4,000-foot level. The day stretched into a daylight evening, and it was nearly dark before they had finished. But once set up they were well equipped. They had a cookhouse, tents, sleeping bags, clothes, food, weapons, ammunition, hunting knives, and dynamite. They had a chain saw, two 2101 Husky power saws, a generator, a propane tank, a drill rig, a forty-five gallon fuel drum of gas, tools, and other assorted equipment.

Over the next few weeks, they would periodically be flown off the mountain, to gather further supplies, replenish their provisions, and then return to the campsite. Each time they left camp they carefully secured their food supplies high in the trees safe from bears. At this time of year, salmon and berries were plentiful so the bears left their camp alone.

But they weren't without further frustration. Jimmy had dowsed one particular location and determined the gold to be at the twelve-foot level. They began drilling, working deeper and deeper. Then at the ten-foot level, the drill bit stopped. Upon examining it, they found that it was working without any problem. Had it hit some impenetrable strata? No, the drill was designed to penetrate anything it encountered to a depth of thirty feet. Just two feet from a vein of gold, by mysterious circumstances, the drill had refused to go deeper. Once again, their thoughts turned to the curse that had haunted them from the beginning. When later they had the drilling rig flown out to be checked, nothing was found to be wrong with it. So what then, if not this strange mysterious force that safeguarded the gold, could explain this mystery?

Along with mystery, they also had their frustrations. Try as they could, it was inevitable that they would need some tool or piece of equipment they didn't have. In one case, they needed to have a sparkplug wrench. When the helicopter arrived, the pilot was given the simple task of flying out to pick up the wrench and bring it back to them. Then, while the pilot was carrying out his mission, they broke the sparkplug. They had no choice but to send the helicopter out to buy the sparkplug and bring it back to them. At the hourly rate of 500 to 600 dollars for the helicopter, it became a very expensive sparkplug.

Each morning around 5:00 A.M. they would rise and start their day with a hearty breakfast, usually bacon and eggs along with hot cakes and coffee. Usually Mark or Kelly would volunteer to make the first of their two daily meals.

The days were long and grueling, often ending only by the fall of darkness. Dinner and much needed sleep concluded their evenings.

Progress was slow, and sometimes disappointing. But by the end of the summer, though they hadn't finished drilling, they had indeed made progress. Summer, however, was gone and by late September as the weather cooled and the approach of winter crept nearer, they were forced to stop. They tidied up the campsite, and stored things away for the winter. Some items could stay but most would have to be flown out. They had gotten very close. Another few weeks or maybe months and they'd reach their goal, but weather was intervening. All they could do now was wait the winter out and hope for an early spring.

With the intention of pulling out the equipment, Jack hired the helicopter to fly him into the camp. Oddly, the updraft of winds caught the helicopter, forcing it to rise steadily upwards in the warm air. Nothing the pilot could do would bring the helicopter down. Unable to land, they abandoned the attempt to recover their gear. That in itself, seemed ominous.

It proved to be just that.

* * *

Her cries for help drifted silently on the wind. She had all but given up hope. Was there no one to hear her, no one to offer help, nothing that would stop the pain she'd suffered? One last time, she called out to the skies and the heavens above.

They were dark and troubled. Restless and forbidding. But at last they had heard her.

They answered her pleas.

At 4:30 A.M. in the dead of night, a single bolt of lightning struck the camp. It ignited a fire that crept toward the forty-five-gallon drum of fuel. In a split second, the drum exploded in an inferno of sound and fury, sending balls of flames in every direction. Fire was everywhere. The heat was unbelievably intense. As the rifles and hand guns were consumed, the boxes of ammunition exploded into what sounded like a Vietnam battlefield. At dawn, forestry workers, rehabilitating from a minimum security prison flew over the camp in hopes of salvaging at least some of the equipment. The flames and fireworks kept them well at bay. They quickly concluded any rescue attempt would be suicidal.

The fire first destroyed the camp and then continued on its way. By 4:30 that afternoon it had turned itself into a raging forest fire out of control.

The entire campsite had been destroyed. Great puddles of metal were all that identified the power saws. Their rifles, shotguns, and handguns had fused together in a warped and twisted heap. Trees had been burned and their stumps had been blown out of the ground with the explosions.

Nothing remained as signposts of their camp.

The mountain sleeps its eternal sleep.

Jack's mountain.

It has been 100 years since Slumach put the curse on his legendary gold mine. With the passage of time, will we see the curse lift and disappear just as it had arrived? Or will the next and final attempt bring to the man who has so relentlessly pursued his dream, his ultimate and perhaps ordained death?

Epilogue

July, 1992. Jack sat across the desk from me, the manuscript pages in one hand, a Coors in the other. Pussywillow lay curled up in his lap as always, eyes half-mast, the purr turned down to a two on the Richter scale.

He was a different man. Forty pounds lighter, he had a tension about him, almost an aura, as if he had entered another world, or witnessed the unbelievable, or lived another life.

He'd spent the last two months on the mountain. His mountain. For the most part alone. And for the first time since I had met him two years ago, he was reticent, vague, unwilling to talk about the mountain. The conversation remained general, polite, and superficial. Maybe he was tired. Yet deep within his blue eyes, a strange fire smoldered as if hinting at an inferno within his soul.

I had seen him tired. I had seen him depressed. I had seen him excited. And I had seen him anxious. Through the endless hours of interviews and taped conversations, through cases of Coors in the long hot summers and the 'gallons of hot chocolate through the dreary damp winters, I thought I had seen his every mood.

I had never seen this.

"Jack?"

"Oh yeah, what was I sayin'?" He'd drifted off again, back into some invisible world.

"The Spaniards...."

"Yeah...my dad and I saw these two arrow markings carved in a tree that pointed across a deep canyon. They were old. Real old. And we found pieces of cable. There were knots tied in the cable...yes, from having rope tied around it...it was the core of the rope...the rope was all gone. And there was a metal bucket frame with dark stuff in between the metal of the bucket's top band that looked like dirt but was old rotting leather."

"And you believe these were left by the Spaniards?"

"Can't see no other explanation. Loggin' don't use nothing like that cable. And minin' don't. Then there's the door we saw carved and all with men wearing armor and helmets on their heads. And my father seen the cave..." His eyes drifted away again. "I think my father maybe seen more than a cave. He just kinda never talked about it."

"And the curse. Tell me now after all the things that have happened over the years, to so many others. Do you believe the curse was ever real? And, if so, do you believe it still exists?" This was the final roundup. The few remaining questions, the final checks on details, the corrections and inadvertent omissions needing to be caught before the book would move to its final stage.

His expression suddenly changed. It was several moments before he answered. "I guess it's kinda hard to believe...when you're all safe and warm and comfortable. Maybe sitting in a chair by a log fire. And it's after dinner and you've watched television for awhile. It's different you know, when you're on the mountain. It's cold, it's rugged, it's lonely. Even hostile. It's kinda like...well it's kinda like you're trespassin' on somethin' or somebody's soul. It's as if you're bein' watched all the time. Sometimes it's as if somethin's whispering right in your ear. 'Course anybody's goin' to say it's the wind, but it ain't. I hear the wind. And it ain't the wind. There's a force. Almost an impenetrable wall that's there. You go so far and then it stops you. Stops you in a way you can't explain 'cause there just ain't no explanation. Sometimes I think I'm goin' to overcome that force... that curse. But sometimes I think its goin' to kill me. Me along with all the others it's killed.

"Do I believe in the curse? Yeah, when you've sensed it, when you've felt it, it's there. And it's real."

I reached out and stopped the tape recorder. Silence filled the room like the sudden apparition of a tombstone.

"Then that's it, Jack. I think we've covered it. I know you don't have much time...you said you're going back in the morning?

"Yeah, the helicopter's flyin' me back in 'bout eight o'clock."

"And you'll call me, just as soon as you've had a chance to read the manuscript through once again?"

"Yep. I'll call you. Let you know just as soon as I get through it."

He stood and slipped the bundled papers into his briefcase. At the door he turned back to me.

"Thanks Elizabeth, for everythin'. I feel good knowin' that someday people are gonna know the story."

There seemed some pleasure in the words he spoke, but they also seemed tinged by sadness. His arm came around me in a final bear hug and then he was gone.

"Call me huh," I shouted after him, "I'll be waiting."

He turned and his arm came up in a salute, then he was gone.

It was early spring of 1993. Bitterly cold, a lifeless sky, a dead world still frozen in its winter sleep. Jack and the two other men anxiously viewed the river and the rapids as they skillfully maneuvered the twelve-foot fiberglass boat around the boulders and rocks in their path. They had traveled eight miles up the river, and the strain showed in their faces and in their posture, rigid with tension. The angry rush of the rapids served as a symphony of sound. The men themselves remained mute. Then suddenly, the bow struck a rock, swinging the boat precariously sideways. A second later the river caught the boat, capsizing it, sending the three men and their supplies into the frigid water.

Instantly chilled to the bone and gasping for air, the men scrambled to shore, catching a glimpse of the overturned boat being carried downstream. The motor was gone as were the cameras, binoculars, and all their supplies and equipment. Jack and the two men, exhausted, frozen, and disheartened eventually made their way back to safety. But countless hours of searching along either side of the river back down to the inlet, failed to provide any trace of anything. Like all those who had trespassed against the legendary curse into this godforsaken country in search of the elusive gold, everything had simply disappeared.